Come Back To Me, Beloved

BOOKS BY
KATHLEEN NORRIS

Come Back to Me, Beloved
An Apple for Eve
Dina Cashman
The Venables
These I Like Best
The Secret of the Marshbanks
The World Is Like That
Mystery House
Lost Sunrise
The Runaway
Baker's Dozen
Heartbroken Melody
You Can't Have Everything
Bread into Roses
The American Flaggs
Secret Marriage
Shining Windows
Beauty's Daughter
Woman in Love
Maiden Voyage
Three Men and Diana
Manhattan Love Song
Victoria: A Play
My California
The Angel in the House
Wife for Sale
Walls of Gold
My San Francisco
Treehaven
Younger Sister
Second-Hand Wife
Belle-Mere
The Love of Julie Borel
Hands Full of Living
Beauty in Letters
The Lucky Lawrences

Margaret Yorke
Passion Flower
Red Silence
Storm House
The Foolish Virgin
What Price Peace?
Beauty and the Beast
The Fun of Being a Mother
My Best Girl
Barberry Bush
The Sea Gull
Hildegarde
The Black Flemings
Little Ships
Mother and Son
Home
Noon
Rose of the World
The Callahans and the Murphys
Butterfly
Certain People of Importance
Lucretia Lombard
The Beloved Woman
Harriet and the Piper
Sisters
Josselyn's Wife
Undertow
Martie, the Unconquered
The Heart of Rachel
The Story of Julia Page
The Treasure
Saturday's Child
Poor, Dear Margaret Kirby
The Rich Mrs. Burgoyne
Mother

KATHLEEN NORRIS

Come Back To Me, Beloved

The American Reprint Company

NEW YORK
1976

Republished 1976 by Special Arrangement
with Doubleday and Company, Inc.

Copyright © 1942 by Kathleen Norris

Library of Congress Cataloging in Publication Data
Norris, Kathleen Thompson, 1880-1966.
   Come Back to me, beloved.

   Reprint of the 1st ed. published by Sun Dial
Press, Garden City, N.Y.
   I. Title.
PZ3.N794Co7   [PS3527.05]   813'.5'4   76-903
ISBN 0-89190-302-X

AMERICAN REPRINT, a division of
The American Reprint Co./Rivercity Press
Box 476
Jackson Heights, New York 11372

*Manufactured in the United States of America
by Inter-Collegiate Press, Inc. Mission, Kansas*

Come Back To Me, Beloved

Chapter One

"You are simply an angel," Paula Hazeltine said absently, panting a little as she dragged the zipper of her evening gown up under her arm. She jerked and smoothed the dress with both hands, watching in the mirror as it fell into place about her hips, frowning slightly. It was not exactly a new dress; it disturbed her to think that it had once been quite loose. That was right after she had had flu, of course. A silly time to buy a dress, for when one got back to normal weight it had the effect of making one feel disgracefully fat! Still, no tiny woman who weighed only eighty-two pounds could ever be called fat!

"I wouldn't go if you paid me," her sister Deborah responded. The two women were alone in Paula's room —a big airy front bedroom such as was suitable to the mistress of the household and the wife of a prosperous lawyer. It was not too neat. The room of the mother of four young children should never, Paula thought, give the impression that it had been picked straight out of a home magazine. But it was comfortable; its hangings of flowered shiny chintz, its bookshelves sheltering *Bambi* and *The Wind in the Willows* as well as more adult fare, its walls hung with many framed photographs, mostly of handsome, serene-looking children.

Paula's nature was serene. It might well be. She had encountered few storms in her forty years; she had many times been taken for her daughter's elder sister and she was innocently proud of her young bloom and unwrinkled cheeks. She looked younger, really, than Deborah, who was actually four years her junior. But Paula was the butterfly type with round blue eyes and corn-silk hair. She had been irresistible as a schoolgirl; no boy had failed to admire her, although naturally many a lad had known from the first that Paula Trezavant would not look at him.

Always first in popularity at school dances and summer outings, always gay and good and safe and protected, Paula had stepped sweetly at twenty into just the right marriage, delighting her father and mother and everyone who knew her, and some who did not even know her, like saleswomen in shops, and librarians and teachers who merely knew that darling, doll-like little Miss Trezavant was marrying that fine young Stephen Hazeltine. And of course they presently had a baby girl with corn-silk hair and then a baby boy and a second baby boy. Three lovely children running around dainty little Mrs. Hazeltine when she was shopping downtown, everybody knowing her and admiring her.

And then years afterward, with some little laughter and even a touch of flushed cheeks and embarrassment, a fourth child, a second girl, had been added to the group, and it was because of little Deborah, called Mimsie by her adoring family to avoid confusion, that Aunt Deborah was staying home tonight. To be sure, Fanny the upstairs girl was in the house, and Wong Foo the cook. But Mimsie had had a little cold and might be wakeful and tearful, and Aunt Deb's offer to stay with her had been gratefully accepted.

"I don't know when I've felt quite so silly as I do going to a dance and opening the cotillion with Steve," Paula said as she delicately fluffed her hair into perfect arrangement and lightly touched cheeks and lips with color. "But of course it's a very special dance."

"You've been chairwoman of the whole thing," her sister reminded her not for the first time, "and you've worked like a little Trojan getting patronesses and managing details. It would be simply terrible if you and Steve didn't go."

"At first," said Paula Hazeltine, more and more pleased with what she saw in the mirror, "it seemed too ridiculous to revive the old cotillions, the 'German' and the 'figures.' But the youngsters have taken up the idea with such wild enthusiasm—— Marlys ought to have this," she interrupted herself to say with a half-reluctant smile of delight as she lifted the soft, exotic beauty of an orchid from its box. She read the card. " 'From the associate workers to a wonderful leader.' You shouldn't have let them do it, Deb," she reproached her sister as she pinned the quivering cluster of blossoms against her shoulder.

"I hated to warn you that they were determined to do it," Deb said. "But I did it because I was so afraid that you'd wear your orange chiffon and spoil it."

"It's lovely on this." Paula looked down at the sweep of her fuchsia velvet approvingly. "Silly, perhaps, to wear a velvet dress to a bazaar . . ." she murmured. Deborah had answered this objection before; she knew what her sister wanted.

"When would you wear it?" she asked. "They'll probably make quite a fuss about you tonight. As far as Marlys goes," she went on, reverting to the previous topic, "she has gardenias from Steve, and that's enough for a first dance."

"In a way it's a first dance, but Marlys has been dancing since she was ten," her mother said.

"Well, her first since the accident then. And you may be sure," her aunt said, "that she'll have plenty of partners. Some of the boys went to see her every three or four days while she was in the hospital. I know Prent did."

"Prent!" Paula Hazeltine said with a slight curling of her lip.

"Prent's awfully nice, Paula."

"I know he is, dear. And I know he's always had a

soft spot for Marlys, since she was a mere baby. But he's just twice her age."

"My age," Deborah said. "It isn't senility, exactly."

"Darling, don't be a fool. I only meant that Prent Talbot seems to Marlys to be in her father's class!"

"She likes him. They did English crossword puzzles together in the hospital. And, after all, he's Steve's junior partner. That makes it rather—suitable," Deb said hesitantly.

"Deborah Trezavant, you're not suggesting that a little gypsy like Marlys seriously considers Prent!"

"I don't know that I am. Physically, I suppose, he isn't attractive. Just a little fat and shapeless and with the everlasting eyeglass," Deborah admitted, laughing. "But he does come of a fine family, and there's stability about him."

"*And* he reads Shakespeare *and* he likes the poets!" Paula supplied with a little sly laugh of her own. "But no," she added, "Marlys is in no mood to pay much attention to Prent tonight! She's simply wild with joy at getting back into the current."

"You know, Paula," Deborah began on a somewhat more serious note, "I'm not wholly sorry that Marlys has had this scare. These weeks of lying still with something to think about, I mean. In the first place, she had no business to be in that car that night—a girl of seventeen. Can you imagine Dad letting us race off thirty miles to pick up some unknown girl who happened not to be able to get to a night club, and then dancing until after one o'clock——"

"Yes, I know. Yes, I know. It was all wrong," Marlys' mother interrupted to admit hastily, her small cameo face flushing. "We've—of course we've all seen that! I never would have let her go if I'd dreamed that it wasn't Tod Smith who was driving or if I'd known that Katy Smith wasn't along. It was all a horrible mistake! Children do terrible things these days, but I've always felt that my children wouldn't. Steve was away and you were away, and she promised to be home on the stroke of midnight. Don't remind me of it! Don't remind me," her thoughts ran on, "of lights in the black night on the drive at two o'clock, and policemen's voices at the door, and the words 'accident' and 'hospital' floating upstairs. 'Your little girl's been hurt, Mrs. Hazeltine——' "

"Am I excited!" said an exultant voice in the doorway. "The thought of the hospital bazaar thrills me as if it were the Stork Club!"

"What do you know about the Stork Club?" But Paula could not hold her voice to a scolding note. Marlys was too lovely to be reproved, especially by her mother. "Somebody looks as if she was going to have a good time tonight," she said.

Marlys Hazeltine came in, silver and white draperies floating about her. A small girl, but taller than her little mother, she was pretty in a puckish sort of way, with a tiptilted nose, round childish eyes darkly lashed like the eyes of a doll, a few pale freckles to accentuate the purity of her skin, crisp red-gold curls tumbled in carefully disordered order all over her head.

"Only tell me I don't look invalidy," she said.

"Invalidy! You're prettier than ever," her aunt said.

"I used to think we oughtn't to tell her that," her mother observed.

"Why not?" Marlys said absently, studying herself absorbedly in the mirror. "A girl knows when she's pretty. And I don't think I'm pretty," she added complacently. "But," confessed Marlys, a dimple suddenly showing in her smooth cheek, "I'd rather look like me than any other girl; I know that. Carol Arnold, *she's* pretty, she's really beautiful. But—fooey!

"I'll tell you," she went on as Aunt Deb sat in pleasant

idleness, watching her, and her mother completed her dressing, "the thing at a dance is just to keep talking, don't you think so, Aunt Deb? Because most boys are shy, and all they want is to have you just keep things going. This is a sort of coming-out party for me, isn't it, Mother? My debut."

"Probably the only one you'll ever have," Paula said with a laugh.

"Aunt Deb!" Marlys pinned her gardenias at a most effective angle. "Did you like dances when you were young?"

It was a stab, of course. At thirty-six one wasn't quite ready for that sort of thing. But Deborah showed no sign of disturbance as she narrowed her eyes thoughtfully and answered briefly, "Some."

"Mother adored them!" Marlys said proudly.

"Mother still does!" Paula Hazeltine laughed. "Come, lambie," she added, "time to get started! Daddy's gone ahead; he's been gone for a long time. He was to pick the Saintburys up at the hotel. Good-by, Deb, and you are a darling!"

"Good-by, and have a wonderful time!" Deb went with them to the front door, saw them depart into the March night that sparkled with late raindrops.

"If it's awful you can always rush to the dressing room and pretend you have to fix your hair!" Marlys said on a final kiss. Her aunt laughed.

"Don't worry. Five minutes after you get there the whole thing will carry you right off your feet," she said. "Remember, it's a bazaar as well as a dance, and you can always wander about selling chances or something. And keep talking!" Deb sang after them. A small boy had dashed out ahead of them to a lighted car that waited in the drive. He got in and started the motor. "Trez, you come back and work at your Latin! Semi-finals next week!" his aunt called.

"Finished!" the boy shouted back. "Dad said I could go into the Hall for a while!"

"You are not finished!" Deborah spaced the words and pronounced them with deliberate emphasis, but the roar of the car drowned them out, and she was left to smile and shake her head, close the big front door, and return to the solitude that, as a member of the big family, she always found welcome.

She put out some lights; the hall light would of course burn on until the return of the merrymakers. But the parlor and living room could be darkened, and when Fanny finished clearing the dining room that would be darkened too. Deb had a word with Fanny, went upstairs to a wide, dimly lighted upper hall, went on for another flight to the big, comfortably shabby room that was occupied by the sons of the family.

A long-legged youth of fifteen was sprawled on one of the three beds, working with some small part of a radio. Sections of the dismembered machine were scattered upon the table.

"Teevy, this is not preparation for midterm finals," his aunt said mildly. She pulled gently from under him the crumpled thin counterpane, folded it expertly, followed suit with the counterpane from the nearer bed.

"Gosh, I'm getting this. It's working!" Stephen Hazeltine junior said, absorbed in what he was doing. "Where's Trez?"

"Driving your mother and Marlys to the bazaar. And he says he may go in for a while."

"He would!" Teevy said in good-natured scorn. "Gosh, you couldn't drag me in there dead!"

"Not even if Phoebe Richards was there, I suppose?" asked Aunt Deb, busily stacking scattered books and gathering up scraps of miscellaneous rubbish.

"Ha, you wouldn't catch Phoebe there, unless there were some sick cats and dogs or a horse or a mountain to climb over!" Teevy said, rolling over, yawning, and sticking his long legs up into the air. "But Marlys—gardenias and slippers—gosh!"

"You wouldn't want your sister to be stoop-shouldered and eyeglassed and interested in the fourth dimension, I suppose?" Aunt Deb said. "Why, it *does* work," she added admiringly as the partly reassembled radio gave forth faint yet unmistakable sounds.

"You bet your life it works!" He jerked himself up and bent over it lovingly.

"Teevy, leave the rest of that until Saturday, that's a darling, and do a little work. Where do you get this rubbish . . . stuff?" Aunt Deb murmured, stacking some pulp magazines whose covers were emblazoned with pictures of gunmen and shrieking women.

"Lots of people read 'em." Teevy dragged his aunt affectionately down and kissed her, tousling her hair. "Is everything you do always admirable?" he demanded.

"Not entirely," said Aunt Deb, breathless and laughing as she regained her feet and pressed her hands against her tumbled hair.

"D'you ever read anything but Shakespeare? Professor Collins says you probably know more about Shakespeare than anyone else in America."

"I don't know how he knows. That would probably mean in the world, if it was true, which it isn't," Aunt Deb said, considering; "for in England they don't make as much of Shakespeare as we do. It's the American tourists who have disinterred Shakespeare, and in Washington we have more folios—I *believe* we have——"

"Professor Collins was here at dinner one night. 'Member? It was one of Mother's amiable attempts to marry you off," Teevy said with a great laugh. "Gosh, what does she care if you marry or not?"

"I've often wondered," Deborah said in her heart. Aloud she said: "When a women is as happily married as your mother she naturally wants her sister to be as happy."

"We'd be in a fine fix here if you married," Teevy observed. "Gosh."

The last word, in its simple fervor, made Miss Trezavant laugh. Before going away with a final plea that he would get to work she placed one more kiss upon the rich black waves of the boy's hair.

The big, roomy house was dark and quiet now in the silence of a spring night. Here and there glints of light crept through from the warm, bright moon that shone over the world or the subdued glow from the hall below and the room next to the baby's nursery. They touched the curved stairway with its delicate spindled railing and the tall, wide white doors. When Deborah, after a peep at the sleeping Mimsie, went into her own room there was no light, but moonshine lay in long-drawn angles on the floor.

She crossed to the window and stood looking out. The garden was whitewashed with brilliance; the barns and sheds and fences that were grouped on a rise of ground at the back stood clear in silver whiteness and inky shadows; the blossoming fruit trees were etched sharply on the orchard earth, and the homely sweet garden below her, where there were roses even now under the oaks and eucalyptus, was dappled with a bright checkering of argent and black.

This had been her father's home; much of her life had been spent under its dormered roof. After Paula's wedding Paula and Stephen had lived for a while in a flowered cottage at the other end of town, but in a few years, when both parents were dead, the sisters had combined forces in the old home, and nowadays the townsfolk often spoke of it as "the Hazeltine house." Deborah did not care. She had in the house no personal pride or sensitiveness. It was sheer pleasure to her that Paula and

Steve and their small girl and boy had come "home" to live, and when Trez and, much later, little Mimsie had been added to the family she had shared their parents' delight. The big rooms needed occupants. Oakover was somehow not a place to witness the sovereignty of a lonesome old maid. It was good to have servants murmuring out in the back garden, a Chinese cook reigning in the kitchen, boys hammering up and down stairs, telephones ringing, Paula always occupied with small garments to mark or alter, birthdays, Christmases, picnics under consideration, friends of all ages coming and going. And it was good to have broad, smiling, even-tempered Stephen for the head of the house, for the years had brought nothing but honor and success to Paula's husband; the town was proud of him and fond of him, and Deborah was too.

"What a night!" she said, looking out upon it. "It's a shame to go to bed!"

But go to bed she did, with that niceness and precision that had been growing on her, only half recognized, in these peaceful years. At thirty-five—no, for ten days now it had been thirty-six, and how old it sounded!—one had one's even routine, deliciously comfortable, and one's luxuries, appreciated afresh every evening.

The tiled shining bathroom, the fat monogrammed towels, the beautiful gifts of many birthdays in silver and Swedish crystal that held creams and powders, the adjusted bedside light, and the awaiting book, these were all things for which to be thankful, and Deborah loved them. But sometimes, contemplating them and all the other beauties that were hers, the velvet frocks in her closet, the warm soft fur coat, the scented delicate handkerchiefs and frail embroidered collars, she had a moment's agony of longing. A young woman's life ought not to be so ordered, so perfect and serene! Children's hands seemed to tug at her immaculate frocks then; visions of her lost country, where porringers were spilled and toys broken, where little voices were shrill, and where a morning newspaper was lowered to show a man's face, grave or smiling, concerned or content, haunted her for a few dreadful seconds.

But they could be banished. She knew how to banish them. She must remind herself that Deborah Trezavant was the angel of the children's convalescent home, that instead of only two or three, hundreds of small hands had been stretched out to her in the last busy years, hundreds of small lives made free of pain and helplessness. She must tell herself that during all these years

Paula's problems had been half solved by her mere presence in the home, and that while Stephen rarely thanked her in words, his eyes, his voice, his quiet inclusion of his sister-in-law in the circle of those he loved most were her reward.

And the children adored Aunt Deb, needed her, turned to her sometimes when they would not turn to their mother. During Marlys' long invalidism it had been Aunt Deb who had carried the brunt of the amusing, entertaining, reconciling.

Then there were books. Their father had left a houseful of books, all the classics of the great English day only a hundred years ago: Dickens and Macaulay and Thackeray and Carlyle, the Kingsleys and Tennyson and Browning. All the poets were there, and the great commentators and critics. And to these Deb had added scores of her own choosing: Scott and Shackleton and Nansen, and the dear dim volumes of Melville and Kane for polar wandering, and two dozen stout, splendid volumes of the Great Mutiny. Then there were old biographies: Sarah Hale and Elizabeth Prentice, Elizabeth Fry and Charlotte Brontë, and among these she could browse inexhaustibly. Deborah spent half of whatever time she had in English or American cities in the old bookstores, sending home treasures to add to treasures, fitting together the tiny pieces of history and building them into a pattern that was never complete.

So that if there were sharp touches of heartache now and then, she could master them, as she mastered a bad moment tonight, took her bath, brushed her thick, soft, tawny mass of hair, settled herself happily in bed with a pile of books beside her.

Francis Thompson; she must look up a special line. And *Winter's Tale*, to reread the delicious bit between the baby prince and the ladies in waiting, and the *The Woman in White*, which she had not looked into for years, and a charming new thing by some French aviator. Deborah laughed as she looked at the collection and wondered whimsically how many pounds of superfluous reading matter she had carted about in her lifetime. Her one deep-seated instinctive terror appeared to be that one might run short of books! Even on picnics long ago she and Tim and Paula had taken O. Henry and Mark Twain and George Eliot along, just in case——

The telephone rang. A startling thread of shrill noise in the quiet night! Queer hour for the telephone to ring! Deborah was conscious of a quickened heartbeat as she reached for her wrapper and went quickly across the hall to Paula's room.

"You'll stop just as I pick you up!" she said to it. But it went on ringing briskly, and she was in time.

A question. Was Judge Stephen Hazeltine there? It sounded like long-distance; someone quite far away was asked if anyone else would do? Where could the judge be reached? came another query in return.

"Well, at the Odd Fellows Hall, perhaps," Deborah said, unfavorably impressed with the manners, at least, of whoever would call up so late. "You can get him at the Odd Fellows Hall," said the operator's impassive voice. Who was speaking? His sister-in-law. Oh well, then, someone would like to speak to her.

"This is Jay Porcher," a man's voice said, clearer and nearer; "please tell Hazeltine I called, speaking for—crik-crik-crik—Singer!"

"I can't hear you clearly!" Deb said more than once. The voice went on inexorably.

"And tell him I'll call him at his office tomorrow!"

One final click. That was the end of that. Deborah looked at Paula's clock: ten minutes past ten. A nice time for anyone to be telephoning! She wrote a message on the pad. Some Mr. Porcher calling Steve about something and would call in the morning at the office. Long-distance. "Sounds very disagreeable," added Deb in her compact, small, firm hand, "and he called Steve 'Hazeltine.'"

"I don't seem to care for you, Mr. Porcher," she said aloud, returning to her room. "My heart doesn't go out to you at all. 'Singer,' eh? Singer. Good heavens!" she interrupted herself, standing still in a moment of dismay. "I hope it isn't that—— She wouldn't, though; she'd never have enough money for a long-distance call! Gracious, I hope she hasn't come back into our lives! Mae Singer. I wonder if that was the name he was trying to say! Well, Steve'll know how to handle it, anyway."

And then for a last thought before plunging into her books, "Oh, I hope my little Marlys is having a wonderful time!"

Odd Fellows Hall was a blaze of light and a sea of music when the Hazeltines arrived. To Paula the conviction came with an immediate rush of pleasure that the bazaar was already a success, that everyone was here—even Yolanda Burns, who had been sneering at the idea for weeks, and old Senator and Mary Saintsbury, who had sent a modest check with regrets that they could not come. No mistaking the atmosphere of high holiday that filled the hall: murmur of voices, laughter, scraping of feet, music, and the smell of popcorn and of the ropes of pine that looped the room. Between the pine loops were banners and flags; Paula had been one of the women who had hung them, climbed ladders with an aching back, driven tacks with fingers stiff with pine gum and dust and paste.

Steve was there, talking earnestly with Senator Saintsbury. Everyone was there, and everyone was glad to see gay, pert little Marlys on her feet again; young masculine arms swung her away from her mother before the first pleasant babble of welcome and congratulations at the door had died away. A waltz was playing. Young girls came up with books of chances. Everyone was moving, smiling, talking.

The big room was partially darkened, and a young man from the stage announced that Miss Lily Breckenridge would sing a selection from *Aïda*.

"Somebody ought to have told him that *Aïda* is three syllables," Paula thought. But she did not stop smiling. She listened to the song and the encore, a sprightly little composition called "Didn't It Rain!" and applauded with the rest. Then she went the round of the booths, smiling and admiring everywhere. The candy-counter girls were in despair. They were just about sold out.

"Jean Forsyth went home and made a lot of divinity and that's all gone too!" they wailed.

"And you had so much! It looked to me this afternoon as if you never could sell it!" Paula sympathized.

"They're going to raffle the cakes," said little Di Briggs.

"Auction them, you mean," Winny Macdonald corrected her.

"I mean auction," Di agreed.

Paula drifted on, presently joined Stephen and the Saintsburys, who were comfortably seated on some of the chairs that were grouped in a corner near the stage. It was pleasant to watch the bright kaleidoscope of the hall; Marlys, Paula noted, was dancing with the Briggs boy. And now with the Richards boy.

"Is that tall boy Tom Richards or is that Larry?"

"That's Tom. Don't they shoot up!" Mrs. Saintsbury's grandchildren were getting up to dancing age now; she thought that if Phil retired this year it would be pleasant to live in Ravenshill again and have young Kate and Rachel grow up here as their mother had. She and her husband were here for only a few weeks now; they had not opened the house; they were at the hotel, which seemed strange. "I like Ravenshill," she said to herself; "it would be very peaceful to be back here, settled down."

There was a lull in the dancing; the second-year-high students were to present three tableaux. A general rustle of expectation went over the hall; the older group in the chairs squared about to get a good view of the stage. Prentiss Talbot wandered vaguely over and took a seat next to Paula Hazeltine. Marlys, flushed and radiant from dancing, came up to drop down in an empty chair on her mother's other side and confess pantingly that she never had had such a good time in her life.

"You look wonderful, Babsie," said Prent.

"Please don't call me Babsie, Prent," the girl said, annoyed. "Everybody else has stopped except you."

"Then it makes it especially my name for you." Prent adjusted the monocle that had been his affectation since a boyhood spent in England and smiled at her through it. Marlys tossed her head and turned away.

"Mother," she said in an undertone when Prentiss' attention was for a moment distracted, "do you see Vera Houston, over there?"

"In the bright red? Yes, and that's young Jim Lane with her, isn't it?"

"He's not young," Marlys said, widening surprised eyes. "He's twenty-eight."

"Well, I mean junior!" her mother conceded, laughing.

"He's crazy about Jean," Marlys said absent-mindedly; "he always has been. Betty-Lou says they're engaged. But I didn't mean them. I meant—— Look! There he goes, walking with Jean Arnold. Look! Over by Mrs. Pope."

"Oh-h-h," Paula said, interested. "Who's that tall boy?"

"That's Condy Cheeseborough," Marlys answered, swallowing.

"Who? Oh, for pity's sake!" Paula said. She touched her husband's arm, and Stephen turned his good broad face toward her. "Look over there with Dr. Pope's crowd, Steve," she said. "Now, talking to Daisy Pope—that's Cassie Ashe's boy. Remember? He was here a few years ago, visiting his aunt and uncle, the Butlers."

"He was!" Marlys exclaimed.

"Certainly. Andy Butler is his uncle, and General

Condy Ashe—— Isn't he stunning!" Paula interrupted herself to say.

"Mother, I never knew that!" Marlys said tragically.

"Knew what, lovey?"

"That he'd been here a few years ago. I was twelve. I was quite old enough——"

"Heavens, Steve, isn't he like Peter!" Mrs. Hazeltine was not listening.

"I wouldn't say anyone was like Peter Cheeseborough," Stephen said in his slow, kindly way. "That's not much of a compliment."

"I only meant in being so handsome, Steve. This looks like an awfully nice boy. Does he dance well, Marlys?"

"Oh, heavens," said Marlys, doubled over, busy with a slipper strap. "Don't think for a minute that Jean intends to let anyone else get a look at him!"

"But I thought you said Jean and Jim were practically engaged?"

"Jean Forsyth."

"Jean Forsyth! How long has that been going on?"

"He's a Yale man," Marlys said, sitting up with a flushed face and straightening her hair with practiced hands; "he's going to be a lawyer."

"Steve, Marlys says that young Cheeseborough's finished Yale and is going to be a lawyer."

"Well, his grandfather'd be pleased with that. I went in with Cheeseborough and Stephenson as soon as I came out of law school," Stephen said. "Ask the boy to come to the house some night, Marlys."

"I haven't met him," Marlys said primly.

"Didn't Jean introduce him?" her mother demanded.

"Didn't—happen to." She was looking far away, with narrowed eyes.

"Well, they can't keep him shut up in anybody's pocket in this town," Paula said comfortably. "There'll be little parties for him."

"Mother! When he's spent all his holidays in New York, you can just imagine what he'd think of little holiday parties in a California town!" Marlys protested. "I'd die rather than ask him to come to our house for pencil games!"

Her father and mother exchanged slightly puzzled and quizzical glances over her head, but nothing was betrayed by her mother's voice as she said smoothly:

"If he's chosen to come here, dear, and practice law with his uncle—I suppose that's his plan——"

"Mother," Marlys broke in in nervous distress,

"please don't have me married off to the man before he's even finished law school!"

"Oh, I thought he had graduated. Then what's he doing here now? Taking last quarter here? Well, that's nice. We'll all give him as good a time as we can."

"We can't chase him, Mother," Marlys said in pained reproof.

"Chase him! Darling, his mother's sister, Amy Ashe, was one of my bridesmaids."

"She was married long before you were, his mother was," Marlys persisted firmly.

"And his aunt Mollie was, too, of course. She was much older than Amy and I. Cassie Cheeseborough died when this boy was quite small and his father married again; they never lived here after Cassie died. I think there are other children now—one, anyway. But he's much handsomer than Peter Cheeseborough ever was," Paula mused.

"How much influence have you with your husband?" old Senator Saintsbury was asking her. Marlys was showing an unwonted interest in Prentiss, and Prentiss' round, smooth face was beaming. Paula squared her chair about to adjoin the senator's chair, smiled inquiringly.

"Well, it all depends upon how much he wants to do a thing!" she answered, with the happy little petted air that made what she said sound charmingly saucy. "If it's duck hunting, I have *none*. None whatsoever. But sometimes, if it's *very* unimportant——"

"Silence, please!" said a woman's clear voice from the stage. The lights went down. Everyone settled into silence and expectation as the tableaux began.

"Paula, have you any plans for Easter? They'll all be home in ten days," someone said pathetically when the hall was lighted again and the enthusiastic applause had died away. Helen Briggs, gray-headed and lean as a hound, had taken Marlys' chair, and Marlys was standing close beside her talking to Jean Forsyth, Jean Arnold, the Briggs boy, and Cassie Ashe's Condy. Marlys looked like a curly-headed child as she lifted her thick dark lashes and tipped back her red-gold mop to stare up at the new man. Paula couldn't hear her, but she knew Marlys could take care of herself.

"I was just asking Mother about you and she said she knew your aunt Amy very well," Marlys' clear little voice was saying shyly.

"I have so many relatives and old friends of Mother's here," the boy answered ruefully, now shaking hands with the senior Hazeltines who had stood up to welcome him, "that I'll not get away with anything, will I, Judge?"

"Well, we'll give you all the leeway we can, Condy," Marlys' father assured him. "Senator, here's the son of an old Californian," he added, introducing friendly old Saintsbury.

"And your aunt Amy's in China," Paula said regretfully.

"Not now. She's in Mexico, and hating it!" Condy answered with his brilliant smile.

"Hating it? Oh, too bad!" Paula said. "Oh, go on talking to him, go on talking to him, keep him here!" Marlys breathed fervently in her soul.

"Well, she loved China; she had a wonderful place there." He tipped his head on one side, spoke deprecatingly, as if apologizing for his aunt. "Uncle René is back in China somewhere, and of course it makes her nervous. You know she has twins?"

"Know she has twins!" Paula said in affectionate reproof. "Of course I do! Between Teevy and Trez. But I've not seen them."

Condy sighed even while his big smile continued to light his brown lean face. A dance was starting.

"No discharge in the war, Jean," he said as the music started. A moment later they had danced away.

"W-a-a-t? W-a-a-t?" Marlys murmured vaguely as her mother and Prentiss spoke to her. Her mother had asked her, if she were not dancing, to watch her purse. Prentiss had said that *she* was dancing and had straightened his tall, usually stooped figure. His tuxedo looked somewhat baggy upon him, Marlys had before this perceived, especially when contrasted with the athletic easiness and young, charming awkwardness of Condy Cheeseborough. Marlys' father was in dinner coat, too, as several of the older men were. Many of the happy husbands and fathers who were dancing or surging about the hall in a ring of children wore business suits or white trousers and dark coats. But Condy was in that costume to which Marlys had only recently learned to refer as "tails."

She always had to dance once or twice with Prentiss because he was Dad's partner. Usually it was an unmitigated bore, but tonight she endured the long stupidity of it without any consciousness of annoyance; it was not really Prent with whom she was dancing.

The Boy Scouts, who had been much in evidence as guides and runners, presently interrupted the music for a patriotic number that brought tears to some of their mothers' eyes. Then it was half-past ten, and the children and many of the parents began to disappear; the crowd thinned, and tiny Shirley McCoy was put up on a table and made to draw numbers from someone's hat for the raffles. The Italian cutwork tablecloth, the vanity chest, the painted mirror, and the standing lamp were all distributed among their lucky winners. But all the chances on the convertible runabout had not been sold, it was announced. They would be on sale all week at Foster's——

"And Pepper and Tubbs'!" a voice called.

"And Shillingers'!"

"Thank you, gentlemen," said young Dr. Fisher. "These tickets, at one dollar apiece, six for five dollars, thirty-five for twenty-five dollars—may represent——"

The music began again in so restfully peaceful an atmosphere, with so much more room on the floor!

"Don't you get tired, little girl? You're only a few weeks out of hospital!" said old Dr. Pope.

"Tired!" Marlys was on wings. To every girl once in her life should come the hour that had come to her— a time when she knew herself lovely and fragrant and young, light on her feet, swirling in a starry cloud of white, passed from one pair of strong young arms to another in a dream of music and soft lights and wheeling colors. It was all laughter, fun, whispering; it was only flying by too fast. The big clock beside the stage ticked on relentlessly; the orchestra would only stay until two o'clock.

But then, after two o'clock, when the hall was deserted except for twoscore boys and girls, the best part of all began. For Ken Briggs had slipped home for his fiddle, and Harriet Willis, the Somers' cousin, turned out to be a marvelous pianist, and the swing began all over again with fresh ardor, and the singing, with them all gathered about the piano trying effects in harmonizing and pressing over each other's shoulders—"Smoke Gets in Your Eyes" and "Old Man River" and the inescapable "Long, Long Trail." Harriet could slip from one to another with a few adroit chords, and she could interpolate dozens of songs that they had half forgotten and sang with all the more gusto.

The spring dawn was pearling a soft sky and birds were singing and fluttering in the trees around the courthouse when Jean Forsyth, Jim Lane, Marlys Hazeltine, Jean and Carol Arnold, and Condy Cheeseborough came out on the steps of the Hall. Marlys' face was pale and radiant; her hair was somewhat disordered and pushed back from her forehead; she looked oddly childlike. Her blue velvet coat—Aunt Deb's evening coat—was muffled about her; she leaned against Carol, laughing and gasping.

"Have a good time?" Condy said, looking down from his great height upon her.

"Oh-h-h . . ." She drew it out endlessly. "I've never had such a good time!"

"Me neither," Jean said, adding simply: "I'm dead."

"Coffee and scrambled eggs at Binney's, ladies?" suggested Jim Lane, who never had enough of a party.

"Our mothers would kill us," Jean said, and Marlys widened her eyes and shook her head.

"We have to go home. It's quarter to four."

"And if we're going into town tomorrow, Condy . . ." Carol said. Marlys' heart did something queer. They were all going somewhere tomorrow—they hadn't asked her—

"Well, gals, who's nearest?" They were all packed into Jim's car now; the downtown streets looked wan and deserted in the struggling lamps and the strengthening light of dawn. "Marlys, you're nearest. All right, next stop the famous Hazeltine homestead, notorious because of the series of murders which so mysteriously——"

"Oh, Jim, shut up!" Jean said, shuddering. "You remind me of the restaurant thing last week."

"An' you fellers let us out of this car!" Carol, who was older than the others and generally considered the comedian of the group, said sharply. "All you says was you was goin' to take us to see your aunt an' maybe give us a coupla cocktails!"

"Oh, I love it," Condy said in an undertone. "Keep it up, for heaven's sake!" Marlys felt a strong pang of jealousy for Carol, who always seemed able to make people laugh. Of course she was twenty-two, which meant she had had some four years more experience than Marlys.

"We ain't goin' to hurt youse gals," he said, encouraging Carol; "keep your shirts on."

But Carol had shot her bolt. With a yawn, poorly concealed, that almost dislocated her face, she collapsed against Jim's shoulder murmuring that she was dying.

They were at the Hazeltine door. Her grandfather's house looked dignified and impressive, even to Marlys' familiar eyes, with the dawn gray, soft, and shadowless on the trees, and the birds going wild in the old-fashioned garden. It was a brick house, painted white, with bay windows flanking the formal columned doorway and a fanlight above the door. As the car stopped a light flashed up in an upper bedroom.

"That's Aunt Deb," Marlys whispered with her laughing good-bys. "Thanks ever so much, Jim, and good night everybody!"

"Chivalry dictates that I accompany you to the door and see that no marauding bands attack you," Jim whispered back raucously. "But if I have to get these Arnold harpies home I'd better be on my way!"

"Oh, don't think of it, Jim. They leave the door open anyway." But when Marlys turned to run up the path and the steps big Condy Cheeseborough was beside her.

Marlys was entirely unable to speak. After one shy and eloquent glance she moved silently beside him; it seemed a long way. Oh, what to say—what to say—what to say!

After all, it was only a few seconds before she opened the door into the soft dim light of the wide hallway and raised her eyes for another smile and managed a "Thank you!"

"Good night, Marlys," Condy said. She watched him as he turned and ran down the steps. His evening wear was somewhat crumpled, but he wore it like a gentleman; his bare, thick hair was tumbled and he was smiling. The lean brown face and the white teeth——

He waved his hand, jumped into the car. The door slammed.

Marlys turned back into the house and went slowly upstairs. She moved like a girl in a dream.

Chapter Two

IN THE PLEASANT SUNSHINE of the breakfast room Paula Hazeltine sat enjoying what was one of the peaceful hours of her day. It was almost nine o'clock; the boys were off to school; Stephen, with his folded newspaper in his pocket, had departed for his office; Fanny had asked about meals. Deb had had a disturbed night with little, coughing Mimsie, Paula suspected; anyway, she had not yet come down. As for Marlys, the family debutante had been so deep in happy dreams when her mother had peeped into her room an hour earlier that there could be no question of breakfast for her. "Dear little Marlys!" her mother thought fondly, looking at her. She was curled up like a tired kitten, with her face still pale from excitement and her dress in a heap on the floor.

It was wonderful to think of Paula Trezavant's daughter coming along to inherit Paula's mantle as a beauty and a belle. Only yesterday Marlys had been stocky and small, a "funny-looking young one," the family dressmaker had bluntly phrased it as she had fitted school middies and pleated skirts upon Marlys' rotund form. There had been years of dental bands for Marlys, and metabolism tests and gym work and diets. And then the motor crash and the hospital weeks, and now this pretty, saucy, flame-headed slip of budding womanhood of whom they all were so fond and proud.

"Nice to have a pretty daughter, Deb," Paula said, smiling as her sister came down.

"I imagine Miss Hazeltine agreed with you last night," Deb returned, nodding at Fanny, who came in with hot coffee.

"I'm afraid that muggins gave you a bad night, Sis!"

"No, she didn't. I got lots of sleep. But she did have a

coughing spell about four, and I saw Marlys come in. It was nearly dawn."

"Dawn? Those rascals! They begged for one more hour, and Tod and Katy were there, so I said yes. Did she have a marvelous time?"

"I wouldn't let her talk. Just kissed her and made her tumble into bed. She didn't even wash her face. But one look at her eyes was enough. She was simply radiant!"

"I hope she didn't overdo. This first time, you know."

"Happiness like that doesn't tire youngsters, Paula. She'll be in a dream all day. The boys were nice to her, were they?"

"They simply buzzed around her. Oh, and, Deb, who d'you think's here? Cassie Ashe's boy, Condy Cheeseborough. He's staying with Mollie Butler. Perfectly stunning fellow—Steve thinks he's awfully like Peter. The girls were all simply flattened."

"Going to stay here?" Deb's blue eyes were full of interest.

"He's come here for a special course this last quarter. It seems he had a heavy cold or a strep throat or something, and the Eastern doctors suggested a visit to Florida or California or somewhere."

Deborah narrowed her eyes speculatively.

"Marlys meet him? I mean, dance with him—all that?"

"Oh yes. She's younger than the Arnold girls, you know, but they took her right in. The whole crowd of them simply ran the dance! But most of the booths were all sold out then, anyway, and the raffling was over, and I for one was mighty glad to get started for home," Paula said.

"And Cassie's boy is handsome, is he? He was rather a rangy small boy. I was in Europe when he was here a few years ago. And Marlys liked him?" Deb added musingly.

"Shame on you!" her sister said, laughing. Deb raised her eyes.

"Not but what you were thinking exactly the same thing, Paula," she said, smiling. "However, I'm making no plans! Only it explains something."

"What explains something?"

"Explains the—the anesthetic that had been administered to my niece while I was helping her to bed last night—or rather this morning," said Deb. "I asked her if she'd had a good time. She just gasped 'Oh, oh, oh!' in a whisper two or three times. Finally I wanted to know if she had an engagement this morning. She was in her nightgown then and she put her arms around me and slowly wheeled me around two or three times and said, 'Oh, you're sweet, I love you!' And after that," Deb finished dryly as she refilled her pink coffee cup, "she reeled into bed, smashed down her pillow and jammed her face against it, and that was that!"

"The darling," her mother said. But her voice was absent now and her thoughts far away.

"Deb," she presently began, "do you know why Senator Saintsbury wanted to see Steve yesterday?"

"Well, I understood they were going to be here only a few weeks on their way to Hawaii, and I suppose he naturally wanted to talk over—— Steve handled the California end of the Lowenberg case, after all. Was there more to it?"

"He wants to know how Steve feels about running for office," Paula said.

"Senator! My heavens! He's going to retire?"

"He's not going to run again."

The sisters looked at each other for a moment.

"They said something about that years ago, Paula. Remember?"

"Yes, I know. But Steve couldn't afford it then. I

wasn't awfully keen for it. We'd just had this place all done over and the new lighting put in——" Paula hesitated, fell silent, her eyes still on her sister.

"You mean you feel differently now?" Deb asked in surprise.

"Well, I don't know," the other woman said, and laughed.

"Does Steve feel differently?"

"I don't know that either, Deb. We talked 'way into the night about it and didn't get anywhere."

"Steve doesn't like politics," Deb objected.

"I know he doesn't. And goodness knows I don't either. I've always said I didn't like Washington, and I've always said nothing would make me move away from here, where the children's schools are and all our old friends and all that. But of course it would be a great honor for Steve," Paula said speculatively.

"It'd mean campaign speeches, Paula. And moving."

"Mary Saintsbury and I were talking about it. She said that if Steve and I went on with Marlys and the baby, we could leave the boys in school here, of course——"

"But, Paula, Steve's built himself up such a magnificent practice here, and in San Francisco too!"

"I know, I know all that. But I was just wondering . . ." Paula thought hard for a moment, frowning into space. "I mean, Marlys is just eighteen," she presently began again, "and I do feel that there's a sort of finish—a distinction about knowing Washington, having lived in Washington. She might meet someone there who would give her a marvelous start in life. I mean, I was just thinking."

"At Marlys' age," her aunt said decisively, "it's her own crowd that counts. She'd be homesick for months, not knowing one soul or what to do with herself."

"Well, I think you're absolutely right!" Paula exclaimed, waking suddenly from a dream. "I've always felt that way, and I don't see why I should feel any different now. And Steve said flatly that he wouldn't consider it. It would cost thousands—perhaps thirty thousand, he said. But of course there're always contributions to a campaign fund," Paula said vaguely. "Everything's going so beautifully for us that it would be sort of silly—— There's the separation from the boys too. I don't know that I could ever come really to parting from them. And when we went East two years ago, before Mimsie was born, he was so frightfully ill in New York and came back looking like a ghost. No, I've really never wanted to consider it, Deb," Paula finished, gaining certainty every minute, "and Steve doesn't. But—I don't know—there's something rather thrilling about going to the capital. Old Phil Saintsbury seemed so sure that Steve could get it."

"With Saintsbury back of him, I should think Steve could. Oh, speaking of Steve," Deborah said in sudden recollection, "he got my message last night? Whoever it was called up—from the city, I should think—anyway, it was long-distance, after ten o'clock at night. People are so outrageous about thinking that because they happen to be awake and up, you must be!"

"Steve couldn't make head or tail of it. He says Jay Porcher is a notoriously crooked lawyer. Steve says that twenty years ago, about the time we were married, he was against Porcher in some streetcar accident case— that is, if it's the same man, and I suppose it is. There couldn't be two Jay Porchers. I can't imagine what he wants with Steve."

"The rest of it was all garbled. But it sounded like— Paula, remember Mae Singer?"

"Heavens, yes! Horrible creature!"

"I thought he said something about Mrs. Singer last night."

"I hope she comes and asks me for something. I hope she does!" Paula Hazeltine said with sudden fervor. "I'll turn her straight over to the police. I won't waste one minute on her! I'm convinced that she took drugs and that she was peddling drugs. No, I'll not get the poor thing into any fresh trouble," Paula went on, softening, "but I don't propose to be bothered with her or to have her around! If you give her five dollars it means that she's writing you one of those eloquent letters asking for twenty, or she wants to leave the children somewhere while she goes to Los Angeles 'on business.' Business, ha! I know just about what sort of business *she's* interested in. But she'd never get a lawyer, Deb. She might bluff about it, but no lawyer would take a case for her. Anyway, what would she have for a case against me?"

"You'd wonder," Deborah mused. "What a tartar she was!"

"Oh no, she was never a tartar. Always gentle and deprecatory," Paula said, hesitating for the right words. "Always so sorry to bother me, and so explanatory. You know she introduced the man who came to live with her as her husband, and then the real husband showed up and actually threatened Steve—as if poor Steve had anything to do with it!"

"Nice for you," Deborah observed dryly. "I only saw her once, you know. That was just before Margaret and I went to South America three years ago, I think. She impressed me very favorably. Clean and quiet, and the children were ducks."

"Those children were her stock in trade, of course. She pleaded her devoted motherhood whenever anyone questioned her about anything. Poor little things. They must have seen some pretty funny goings-on in dear Mama's home. Dragged about and exploited!"

"But what's she been living on since you stopped helping her, Paula?"

"I don't know and I don't care. Maybe her husband —if either one of those men was her husband—has been supporting her. Maybe she's in an—an older business," Paula said with a significant little laugh. "Anyway, Steve got your message and I suppose he'll tell us tonight what this weasel Porcher was bothering him for."

There was a silence filled with the pleasantness of leisure and harmony in the breakfast room for a few minutes. The toaster was cold now; the coffeepot was cold. But both sisters had long finished breakfast and were interspersing their talk with glances at the morning papers. Inside the little square glass cubicle that was the breakfast room were gay curtains of glazed chintz, wicker table and chairs, pink china, and shining silver. Outside, although this side of the house was in shadow, there was promise of a warm and cloudless day. Lilacs were in heavy bloom; hawthorn trees lifted plumes of pink and white against the dark foliage of the oaks; cinerarias were already disputing the borders with the pansies and primulas of March.

"Well, I must get started. Directors' meeting at ten," Deborah presently said.

"I must get started too. I told Fanny I was going to let Marlys sleep, so she can clean up in here. . . . Wait a minute, Deb."

The last words were added with an effect of impulsiveness, after manifest hesitation. Deborah, who had half risen, sank back in her chair and looked at her sister expectantly.

"I heard this last night from Mary Saintsbury," said Paula, "and I didn't know whether to tell you or not. But I think you ought to know. They have a place near Boston, the Saintsburys have, I mean. And the Washburns lived right near them. And she says that Marcia Washburn died last autumn. It was before Thanksgiving, anyway, because they felt so sorry for him—

even though she says they hardly know him—that they asked him to Thanksgiving dinner. So it was before that."

Deborah sat motionless, looking steadily at her sister. The color had drained from her face and she looked suddenly tired and helpless and young. She swallowed visibly before she spoke.

"D'you believe it, Paula?"

"Oh yes, because it was an accident. It was in the paper. Mary said she'd been ill for months; in the hospital ever since last summer, I think she said. But he wrote them a note, about the Thanksgiving invitation, and thanked them, and spoke of his recent loss—so that proves it."

"Wouldn't the papers have had it here?" Deb asked, her face as expressionless as that of a statue.

"Not necessarily, I suppose. Or we might have missed it. Mary was surprised that we didn't know."

"He would have let me know," Deb said in a half whisper. She did not look at her sister.

"That's what I can't understand," Paula returned. And somewhat timidly she added, "Deb, is it still—I mean, it still matters—it's still so bad?"

"He didn't write me," Deb said half aloud, speaking

to herself. "Yes," she answered her sister vaguely, abstractedly, "it's still—what it was always. It's still—even after eleven years—so bad. For me, I mean; perhaps not for him. He's been working there at the university—meeting other people. But I—I——"

The words came harder and slower. She stopped.

"He treated you terribly," Paula began. "I think he treated you terribly," she repeated.

"No," Deborah said without resentment. "We fell in love. We were in a fools' paradise for a few weeks. But when he went back—she was his foster sister, after all, and her mother had been the only mother he ever knew. He couldn't—I don't suppose he possibly could have broken off with her, when the mother had died, when she was all alone."

"And when he knew she was cuckoo," Paula supplied simply. Deborah laughed unwillingly, mirthlessly.

"She was never an institution case," she said.

"That's the worst kind," her sister stated grimly.

"I've never been sorry," Deborah began again after a minute. "We had those weeks. We had those weeks of fooling ourselves. We had the dance at the country club and the 'Rose Waltz.' "

"I knew you wouldn't change, thanks to our mixture

of Irish, American, and Spanish blood," said Paula. "But I never thought he would either. I'll never forget his face—of course he was the most romantic-looking, Byronic creature God ever made!—that last night, or his saying to me at the door, 'God willing, I'll be back!' It was like the face of a man with his hand in a fire."

"Fire," Deborah said under her breath. "It did one thing for me, Paula," she presently added. "It showed me what I could feel for a man. It kept me from satisfying myself with anything——" Her voice fell. "Anything less," she finished in a whisper, looking away.

"There's no reason why you shouldn't have married anyone!" Paula said. Deborah was not listening.

"This—this upsets me!" she said restlessly, rising and gathering her letters together. "I—I suppose I've been thinking—oh, no matter what! It upsets me."

Paula looked after her wistfully as she went upstairs.

Deborah attended her directors' meeting, handling the task of chairwoman with accustomed ease; she was the sort of slender, quiet, capable person who was always immediately made chairwoman of everything. A hospital wing costing half a million dollars was to be built onto the babies' home. Would it take paying patients? Miss

Trezavant thought it should. How about mental cases?

Adelaide Ruffers, who always had a pathetic case on tap, made a stirring appeal for the mental cases. She had a friend whose child was perfectly beautiful, but the poor darling——

Miss Trezavant thought that unless they could get a much stronger staff than they had at present they had better not plan to burden "the girls" with mental cases. The vote showed a unanimity for the paying patients; the mental matter was shelved for the present.

It was a delicious warm day, almost too warm. Gardens were in a riot of early bloom everywhere; blossoming hawthorns lined the shady sidewalks. Deborah walked home to lunch with Teevy and Trez, afterward went up to Marlys' room to remind her that Diana wanted her to telephone without fail before three o'clock. Di was having some pictures taken, ostensibly for her mother's birthday but with a suspected reference to the bureau in Juddy Carter's room at the Naval Academy too.

Marlys was awake, enjoying coffee and rolls. She pushed the tray away when Deborah came in, stretched up her bare arms from the wisps of satin and lace that were her nightgown, and gave her aunt a great hug.

"Oh, what a glorious sleep!" said Marlys. "Sit down, darling. Where's everyone? Where's Mother?"

"Mrs. Briggs is having a lunch for Mrs. Petrie; she's on here for a few days from Detroit. Well, did you have a good time?"

Marlys, having communicated with Diana, who apparently was also just waking up, clashed back the telephone, settled back on her pillow, and smiled dreamily.

"Nobody," said Marlys solemnly, "ever had such a time! Everyone—everyone wanted to dance with me, and those older girls—Carol and Vera and Betty-Lou—they were simply angelic to me!

"And we'd walk out on the terrace, at the back," she went on, "and everyone would be walking up and down, laughing, and looking up at the moon. Oh, it was such fun! And Jim Lane—he's so crazy!—he and Jean dancing the craziest way you ever saw! And this Forsyth boy—you know, their cousin; I've seen him about three times in my life—saying to me right before them all: 'Shall we tell them our pretty secret, Marlys?' And of course they all roared.

"At the beginning it was sort of mixed up with kids and the booths and the raffles and things, and of course Miss Breckenridge singing the way she does, as if her throat hurt her. But afterward, when everyone went away— Oh, goodness!" Marlys finished, relapsing into roseate recollection.

"And this new boy, Condy Cheeseborough? Nice?"

Marlys' eyes moved to her aunt's face. She did not smile or speak. Her perfectly steady look rested for a moment, then she looked away.

"Didn't like him?" Deborah ventured, suspecting the situation.

Marlys did not answer for a moment. She narrowed her eyes and looked into space.

"Aunt Deb," she said then seriously, "you believe in love at first sight, don't you?"

"Well, not quite, perhaps." Deb hesitated. "Yes," she amended it, "in a way I do."

"I know I'm only eighteen," said Marlys, "and I know that Mother would laugh at me, and the boys— oh, the boys would love it!" she added with scorn. "But I want to tell you. Now, I'll die if you tell anyone else!" she broke off to say with sudden feeling.

"I won't tell anyone else."

"After a few years," Marlys said, "perhaps you'll believe me. But I don't really care if anyone believes me or not. It just—I just—it took my breath away—I've not been able to breathe——"

"I know," Deborah said. She left her chair and came over to the bedside and knelt down, and they locked fingers. "Poor little Marlys!" she said.

"When I first saw him," Marlys said, her heart bursting with the need to talk about him, "something—you're going to laugh!—but something just seemed to hurt me—like a pain somewhere. And it hasn't stopped since."

"Dance with him?"

"Twice. He's twenty-eight. He was wearing tails," Marlys confided simply.

"And he dances well?"

"Oh, divinely. He's Yale, you know. Yale, imagine! But it wasn't the dancing. It was—he's tall, and his arms just seem to lift you up and hold you so lightly—and he's—he's got an air of saying, 'I'm a man and you're a girl—you're all girl, soft and sweet and right here jammed up against my heart!' " She stopped, suffocating.

"It sounds like the real thing," Deborah said, smiling.

"Oh, Aunt Deb," the girl pleaded, "say it is! Don't think it's just first love that doesn't amount to anything. Don't tell me I'm too young and that I'll be over it someday."

"No, I won't, Marlys."

"I mean," the girl said, "that it's—it's something I'm not ashamed of. I'll never be ashamed of it! He'll never look at me, I know that. Don't think for a minute I have any doubts of that! Why, he's old enough for Helen Brigham, as far as that goes, or Elinor. But that doesn't make any difference, not the least. It was just—just *meant* that I should meet him, and—and dance with him, and feel this way."

For a moment Deborah studied in silence the passionate, exquisite little face so near her own.

"You don't believe me?" Marlys challenged her.

"Yes, I do. Yes, I do," Deborah said.

"At the end, you know, the room was all dark, with those lights wheeling over everything—oh, this was nearly three o'clock. And the Somers' cousin—she's perfectly darling; she's married, but her husband's in the Philippines or somewhere—played the piano and Ken Briggs got his violin, and they played for us. They played the 'Rose Waltz.' "

"The 'Rose Waltz!' " Deb echoed. "I knew old Luigi always played it; he used to play it when I went to dances, years ago. But I didn't know you kids liked it."

"Ken plays with the orchestra sometimes. Anyway, he

knows it. And that was the last dance," Marlys said, "and that was the dance I had with Condy Cheeseborough. And while we were dancing he said, 'You like me, don't you?'"

"And what did you say?"

"I don't think I said anything, much. But then he said——" Marlys stopped abruptly.

"Go ahead."

"It's the—the way he says things!" Marlys began again. "A sort of careless, sure-of-himself way! Like a—like a man. He said—sort of teasing, like a big brother—'Don't you like me too much, now! I'm ten years older than you are.'" She was silent a moment, smiling at her aunt with a shamed, radiant face. "I kept thinking of it all night," she finished simply.

"That was the last dance?"

"That was the 'Rose Waltz.' After that Mrs. Willis said that she really had to go, and we all sort of gathered around and sang for about half an hour—she kept saying it was too late, and then she went and we came out on the steps and looked across at the courthouse, and in the east the sky was all getting pale. Aunt Deb," Marlys said, tragic and earnest again, "what shall I do? I think of him all the time. The telephone rang a few minutes ago and my heart just about suffocated me. He won't pay any attention to me; he thinks I'm only a kid, and some other girl will get him, and I'll—I'll just not bear it! I'll have to go away."

"Oh no, you won't," Deb said soothingly. "It seems to me you've made real headway, considering that you just met him. His aunt Amy is one of my closest friends; she was one of your mother's bridesmaids. It would be very strange if we didn't invite him to this house; we'd have to do that even if you weren't any older than Mimsie. We'll have a little party—nothing formal—at Easter; that's in two weeks now. Or perhaps your mother—I wonder——"

"What?" Marlys demanded eagerly as the other paused.

"I was wondering if we might have a little coming-out party, perhaps in the garden, along about the first of May. Remember we planned that for November, just before your accident? After all, you're eighteen, and after all, you'll have to come out sometime. How would you like that? That would give us a chance to have everybody here and perhaps make a little special fuss about Cassie Ashe's boy."

Marlys' face became slowly irradiated.

"Oh, but Mother wouldn't!" she gasped.

"I think she would. It would be so much easier and simpler than a winter party, for one thing; the gardens are getting lovelier every second. Now listen, Marlys," Deborah said, serious but smiling, "I'm not conspiring to trap Condy Cheeseborough, remember that! He *is* ten years older than you are, and he probably does think of you as a very young girl! But this means we'll see him, we'll find out what sort of boy he is, and of course —*if* you like each other——"

There was a moment of silence during which Marlys kept an adoring gaze fixed upon her aunt.

"You're the kindest person anyone ever had for an aunt," the girl said then. Tears stood in her eyes; she smiled as she winked them away. "Aunt Deb," she began again suddenly, "d'you know what I was thinking last night?"

"About him, I suppose?"

"That I'd like him to be poor, so that I could cook for him and take care of him," Marlys said in a shamed, happy rush; "and that I'd like to have everyone—all the girls—pitying me because we hadn't anything—

feeling sorry for me, and I feeling so rich just because it was us two! And I thought, if we had children, a little girl and then a little boy——

"You've felt that way?" she asked in the moment of silence.

Deborah laughed.

"Yes, I've felt that way. That's—authentic," she answered. "Only I was seven years older than you are when I fell in love. I was twenty-five. There's a difference. Girls do fall in love at eighteen. It could happen. Only it doesn't very often. But you must play your hand very carefully now, Marlys," she warned the girl half seriously. "You mustn't show anything. You must be just yourself, natural and simple and friendly. Not in a hurry. And not ashamed of the boys and Mimsie; your family's all part of your background. If Condy comes here don't try to shove everyone into the upstairs rooms; take him right into the family. Do you understand?"

"Oh, I will!" Marlys promised fervently.

"And come to me in three weeks and say, 'Why did I ever think I liked him, just because he was a newcomer and so handsome!'" Deborah said, getting to her feet. Marlys had locked her hands behind her head; her eyes were half closed. She was lost again in dreams.

Presently she got up and dressed and telephoned Jean. The pleasant routine of a warm spring day went its accustomed course. Mimsie waked up from her nap, one small cheek very red, was put down in the garden in her play pen and watched by Georgia Edwards, plain, gentle, forty, disillusioned, who came over every day for the express purpose of watching Mimsie. Aunt Deb came and went, sharing the responsibility; Paula appeared on the lawn at five o'clock with her knitting, asked Georgia a few questions about her invalid son and runaway daughter. Queries about Bessie had to be carefully framed. Georgia's husband had deserted her years earlier; her son Stuart had been injured and would be helpless for life; Bessie had recently eloped with a married man, and nobody knew quite what Bessie's future plans were. Paula felt heartily sorry for Georgia; the contrast in their fortunes was glaring, yet as little girls in grade school together Georgia's prospects had seemed as bright as those of Paula Trezavant. Paula did all that she could for her.

The spring afternoon was soft and warm. Oaks threw a gracious shade over the lawn; it was too hot, in the third week of a California March, to sit in the sun. Paula could smell lilacs and acacia; tiny gold acacia tassels powdered the brick walks. The big house, with its open windows and with the trembling shade of the tall pear trees falling in a delicate pattern on its mellowed white brick, looked substantial and homelike. When Deborah came out Paula told her that this was the sort of day that made one glad to be alive.

Deborah, whose thoughts all day long had been utterly confused, nevertheless agreed.

"For some reason these days always make me think of us as children," Deb said. "I mean these first really hot, enervating days. Remember Grandma Trezavant in those black taffetas, going around the house reading letters from old friends to Mother, no matter how busy Mother was?"

"I don't suppose any old lady writes as many letters now as Grandma did."

" 'Mary, I've just had such a sweet letter from Harriet Stone. They're all down in Florida and she writes such a sweet letter about it,' " Deb quoted.

"Harriet Stone! I haven't thought of her for years. . . . We're out here, Marlys!" Paula called. Marlys, flushed and warm, came from the front gate and dropped into a basket chair.

"Hot," she said, panting.

"Where've you been, dear?"

"I walked over to Di's and we went to the Fair; a heel came off her slipper last night and she wanted a pair of tennis shoes anyway."

Marlys did not say that the suffocating thrill of the walk had come to her when they passed Odd Fellows Hall. The doors—those weather-blistered doors that had looked so glamorous in moonlight last night—had been wide open to hot afternoon sunlight today; men had been carting away the skeleton supports of the booths. Here and there twisted bunting and silver paper clung to the raw, thin boards; these draggled reminders had been enough; the mere sight of them had brought back the evening's bliss and pain in a rush.

"See anyone else?"

"No, we were going to the Arnolds'. But they were all in the city today."

"Your mother and I have been talking about a May party," her aunt said.

"I think it would be a lovely idea," Paula approved; "and as we haven't done anything since your accident, it would give us a chance to get rid of some obligations. It wouldn't hurt Steve just now, either," Paula added with a significant glance toward Deborah.

"Daddy—what about him?" Marlys asked alertly.

"You may as well know, because I'd really be glad to know what you think about it, Marlys," her mother said; "they're thinking of asking Dad to run for senator. Senator Saintsbury's retiring, and they feel Dad would be a good man."

"Dad!" Marlys' face brightened for the few seconds it took the idea to dawn upon her, darkened again. "But, Mother, we'd have to go to Washington," she said.

"And you wouldn't like that?"

"Well, I—I wouldn't know anyone there. I remember when you took me to New York when I was fifteen," Marlys said. "I was perfectly crazy to go, and I boasted to all the other girls. But when I got there I was so homesick all I did was write to Jean and Di. I—— Does Dad want to?"

"I don't know, quite. He's thinking about it; I'm not sure how he feels. They talked of it about six years ago; I know we were both against it then. It costs money to run for office, and of course he mightn't win."

"Who'd run on the other ticket? That would really make a difference," Deb contributed.

"Joe Fenelli ran last time. Senator Saintsbury thinks he'll run again."

"But he was a bootlegger, Paula! At least that's what they said."

"That's one of the things Steve hates about politics. Such horrid things are said," Paula said mildly. "Nothing—ugly, has ever touched us," she added, "and I'd rather hate to see Steve plunge into it. After all, the Hazeltine name stands for something. Is that arrogance, Deb?"

"Not among ourselves," Deborah conceded. Paula, here in her old walled garden, was safe from the ugly whispering and snarling of the world. To Paula it would seem only natural that all the good things of life should come this way; there would be a garden party for Marlys—all flowers and laughter and the flutter of spring frocks; handsome young Condy Cheeseborough would fall in love with Marlys, and Marlys marry young and safe and happy, as her mother had. Stephen would presently be sitting here under this great oak, to be photographed for the Eastern weeklies; the new senator from California. Left to right: son, Stephen junior; daughter, Mary Elizabeth; the Senator; Mrs. Hazeltine; daughter, Deborah; son, Trezavant.

But this day, on which mother and daughter, idling under the trees, were lost in happy dreams, was etched in agony upon Deborah Trezavant's heart as if with acid. She would never forget it. All day long the sunlight had seemed to her to wear a brassy color as if it shone through yellow glass; all day long she had turned from solid food because it tasted in her mouth of ashes and she could not swallow it. Barry Washburn free at last and she had not heard from him!

It was to be the last day that Paula and Marlys could dream their innocent dreams of future love and glory, power and change. Deborah could not know that. She could not know that her own personal anguish was shortly to be lost in concern for them. But it was as if she felt now a chill breeze run along the new sweet grass, saw a cloud gathering slowly over the garden.

"Nobody's true if Barry Washburn isn't," she said in her heart. "All these years—when Marcia was living, dragging about the house, whispering to herself, asking him who she was, where she was, who he was—he belonged to me more than he does now. Five months since she died, and he hasn't written me, he hasn't come! And I've kept alive for that; I've kept from going mad because of that! And now it's all gone. I've remembered all these eleven years. He hasn't. Men don't. And why help poor little Marlys into a love affair just to have her face this someday?"

And she looked with a strange jealousy, almost with a moment's dislike, at little butterfly Paula, so young at forty, content, secure in the old home garden, with a beautiful daughter beside her, an exquisite baby drowsy in her lap, two great sons, and a devoted husband presently to come home and spoil her.

But even as she moved her glance away with a little prick of shame, the cloud darkened over the old house, and the moment was gone forever. Stephen's car moved beyond the hedge, stopped at the side gate; Stephen came in, bringing with him a strange man. Or was he quite strange? Something about the dark, foxlike face seemed familiar to Paula, at least.

Stephen looked annoyed, bewildered. He performed brief introductions, nodded to Marlys. Mr. Porcher.

"Will you take Mimsie upstairs? Isn't it her suppertime?"

"Almost," said Marlys, bewildered too. For there was something uncomfortable in the air. She went away with the baby, and Stephen, indicating with a nod an empty chair for the newcomer, sat down heavily.

"Mr. Porcher," he said to his wife and sister-in-law, "is here in the interest of Mrs. Singer. Remember her, Paula? Of course you do. He prefers to settle this matter with me alone. I prefer to ask you and Deborah to clear up his mind about it. I've told him she was a charity case of yours and that she seemed at first a nice quiet woman."

"I wouldn't make any reflections upon her, Mr. Hazeltine," Mr. Porcher said quietly.

Paula, the quick blood in her face, looked in stupefaction from one to the other.

"What about her?" she asked. "We've done—we've done absolutely all we can for her. I've told her that!"

Jay Porcher looked questioningly at Stephen, as if he doubted the wisdom of admitting the ladies to this conference.

"It's a little different from what you think, Mrs. Hazeltine," he said. "Mrs. Singer claims, and we are prepared to prove her claim, that her youngest child, now two years old, is Mr. Hazeltine's daughter."

Deborah and Paula looked at each other a moment in amazement, then burst out into half-angry laughter. But when Paula's eyes went to her husband's face he was not laughing.

Chapter Three

THERE was a long minute's silence of bewilderment in the garden. Paula and Deborah stopped laughing; their angry amusement changed to puzzlement and uneasiness. Jay Porcher, a thin dark man with nervous hairy hands, looked from one to the other. It was Stephen who next spoke.

"Mr. Porcher naturally felt that this affair was something I'd want to keep from you, Paula," he said. "I wish you'd give him an idea of what the real situation is."

"You mean about Mae Singer?" Paula asked with just a touch of impatience in her voice. "Why, she—she simply was one of my charity cases. I brought her here from New York—at least I sent her the money to come and bring her children, and Judge Hazeltine and I gave her a little place we have down toward Santa Clara to live in. A little farm. But she turned out to be quite a different person from what we thought—she drank, and she had men there, and I'm convinced that she not only used drugs but sold them——"

"You naturally have no proof of that," said Jay Porcher as Paula hesitated with a glance toward Stephen.

"We know she used drugs, don't we, Steve?" she said.

"Might as well leave that out. What the authorities complained of was that she was an unfit guardian for her children," Stephen said moderately, not looking at his wife.

"Why, but—why, but——" Paula was amazed at his restraint. "Well, anyway," she resumed, "the children weren't being sent to school—two of them were of school age, anyway, and she kept shifting about from house to house, saying that this man was her husband or that that one was, and finally I told her I was done with her, and we rented the farm to other tenants. I believe she left a box of papers there and some victrola records; I know she wrote me an impudent letter about them afterward, and that was the last I heard of her."

"Suppose we go back to the beginning, Mrs. Hazeltine," Mr. Porcher said suavely. "How did you meet Mrs. Singer?"

"I was coming out of a movie with my daughter three years ago this March—we were in New York with Judge Hazeltine and he had some nightwork to do," Paula answered. "It was raining hard, and this woman was standing under the theater marquee—or whatever you call it—looking very poor and distressed, but not begging. The little boy—Edgar; he was about ten, I suppose—said to me suddenly, 'Mama lost her purse,' and of course I asked her if it was true. She said with a smile, 'There was not much in it, but it would have gotten us home!' and immediately I made her borrow something—fifty cents, I think it was—from me. She asked where we were staying and I told her the name of the hotel and she said she would mail the money to me the next day. But the next day she came instead; she was waiting in the lobby when Marlys and I came down, and we talked."

"She met your husband that day, I believe?" said the lawyer.

"Yes, she did. Steve was as favorably impressed with her as was I. Marlys and I went to see the place where she lived—a miserably poor part of town, black hallways and smells and dreadful plumbing—and she said that her husband was in a hospital for consumptives, but that his old employer—he had been someone's chauffeur—had arranged for a pension of fifty dollars a month for her. She said the Charities could do nothing for her because she had this help, and that her rent was twenty-two dollars. She had nothing more.

"The house was so clean and the children were so nice," Paula went on, somewhat bewildered still at the seriousness with which Stephen was attending this familiar story, "that it rather haunted me. I spoke to Stephen about the Santa Clara farm, the sunshine and fruit and fresh air for the children, and the day before we left I spoke to her. She said it was like the opening into heaven, after the blackness and dampness of the slum she lived in, and that she could get the fare—they would come by bus, they would hitchhike, but they would get here! Stephen very generously gave me a hundred dollars to pay their railroad fare——"

"I think," Jay Porcher interrupted, "that the check was made out directly to Mae Singer."

"I think it was," Paula agreed, more and more uneasy at the man's manner and Stephen's intent air. "It doesn't matter. She and the four—no, it was three then. She and the three children came out a few weeks later. We had partially furnished the house; she bought other things, and for a while it worked. But in a few months she took the whole crowd off on a trip with some man she had picked up. Then in the autumn she told me the fourth child was coming, and I knew that she was not the sort of woman she had represented herself to be."

"So you abandoned her, with four small children to feed and no income whatsoever?" Jay Porcher said.

"Indeed I didn't abandon her," Paula said, flushing. "I went to see her all that winter, argued with her, took her things for the baby. But the baby wasn't two months old before she went off again, taking only the eldest girl and locking the others in the house."

"And that was the occasion when you broke into

her home," Mr. Porcher supplied, looking at notes.

"The Children's Aid 'broke in,' as you call it," Paula said resentfully. "When I got there Miss Christensen was already in the house. They took charge of the children."

"And you rifled her desk?"

"She had no desk! The place was in a perfect mess," Paula answered. "Dishes, dirt, baby clothes, some of the plumbing broken. We looked about to see if we could find out anything about her. By that time we knew that what she had been telling us wasn't true."

"There was no fifty dollars a month from the old employer, for one thing," Deborah supplied. "I was with my sister when she went into the house, and Miss Christensen was also there. We hadn't the slightest idea where Mae was or how to get hold of her. We looked at letters and accounts—anything we could find —for a clue."

Paula looked at her sister in relief and gratitude. She needed support. A glance at Stephen's face was reassuring too. He looked undisturbed, sleepy, half amused. A wave of confidence went over Paula.

"We discovered," she said more firmly, "that her real husband was living in New York, having made no effort to find out what had happened to her. It seemed—to my sister and to my husband and me—to relieve us of any further responsibility. The children stayed with the Associated Charities for several weeks, then she reappeared one day with a man she called her husband, said that he had a good job, and that they were all going to Los Angeles. That's the last I've heard of her, except that she wrote me once that some papers and victrola records had been left at the Santa Clara house and asked for them."

"What was the date you brought her out here, Mrs. Hazeltine?"

"Well—let me see. Deb, you were in Rio with Margaret. Marlys was fifteen—it was about three years ago."

"The month, please?"

"We were in New York in March, and I believe she came on in April or May. I know it was spring."

"And when did all this break up? Give me the events in their order, please."

"It was about September, I think, when I first began to suspect that things were queer. She told me garbled stories of being obliged to go East to see a lawyer—she actually started once with a man neighbor in his car. She said her husband had died, and when I asked for proof she put me off; this went on for some weeks. Then suddenly she broke down and said she had been a silly girl—she always spoke of herself as a girl—and that she had been led away into a friendship under promise of marriage, while supposing her husband dead, and that there was to be a child.

"That completely disgusted me with her, combined with all the rest—the dirtiness of the house and the neglect of the children," Paula finished. "But I did try to go on. As I say, I went to see her, befriended her, and tried to advise her. Her baby was born in April. In June I took my own children to the lake, and when I came back she had completely disappeared. She wrote from Los Angeles, not asking for money, not giving me any news, and I was glad to be rid of her!"

And Paula sat back a little breathless and glad to be done with her story.

"That's my wife's side of it," Stephen said with an air of brevity.

"I don't know what ridiculous representations she may be making," Paula said, reinforced, "but she was simply a charity case of mine—a wretched woman from a slum for whom I tried to do something for the sake of the children. That's all there was to it!"

"You don't think I've come here in my client's interest to believe all that?" Mr. Porcher asked, turning toward the man of the house.

Stephen flushed, but he spoke quietly enough.

"I don't care what you've come here to do or what you haven't!" he said. "I think you've gotten about all that we can contribute to this affair, and I'll be obliged to close this interview. Thank you, dear," he said to Paula. "I wanted Mr. Porcher to hear this from you, just as it happened."

"You had no idea of your husband's friendship for Mrs. Singer?" Mr. Porcher asked Paula. Paula distained to answer; she looked patiently at Stephen.

"You did not know that this youngest child—Claire-Elise Singer—is your husband's child?" the visitor persisted. Deborah and Paula were both on their feet now, and they turned away and walked slowly to the house without speaking. But when they got upstairs they were at no loss for words. Stephen, joining them a few minutes later, interrupted a river of talk.

"Steve! What on earth do you make of this nonsense?"

Stephen sank into a high-backed chintz chair, smiled wearily.

"What do you think of your gallivanting husband?" he countered.

"Oh, don't laugh about it! But, Steve, how perfectly horrible! What *nerve!*"

"They can't do anything, can they?" This was Deborah, her blue eyes indignant. "I mean—you can't blackmail a married man on breach of promise? After all, she was married too. And what I'm wondering is, where is she ever getting money enough to hire a lawyer?"

"Well, it's the darnedest thing I ever heard of," Stephen said simply. "This feller came in this afternoon; he and I had a run-in years ago, before we were married, Paula—and we smashed his case to pieces. As I remember it, the case was thrown out. He came to me this afternoon and demanded my support of some child; I didn't know what he was talking about for fifteen minutes! Then I asked him what he had to go on. He said letters—witnesses——"

"Steve, she never had a letter from you!"

"Never. I asked him if he'd seen them. He said he had several already in his possession and that Mrs. Singer had sworn that others had been destroyed by my wife when she rifled the home."

" 'Rifled the home!' " Paula echoed.

"If you could have seen the home," Deborah contributed. "Babies filthy, stove cold with ashes streaming out of it, clothes and dishes and dirt everywhere! And we—Paula and I—hunting around to find some clue as to where the dear little housemother had taken herself!"

She and Paula laughed in exasperation and relief.

"The real trouble is," Deb said then, sobering, "that Mae Singer is such a respectable-looking, convincing woman. We were completely taken in by her, Paula, and I'm not surprised that anyone else is. What with that demure air and that clear, cool skin and those tearful eyes, she can make anyone think anything. But this is what I want to know, Steve," said his sister-in-law; "suppose the worst. Suppose you *had* had an affair with her—shut up, Paula, I'm just hypothecating this! —I say even if what she says were true, what earthly claim would she have?"

"She wouldn't have any," Stephen answered, "but she could make an awful nuisance of herself. This shyster Porcher told me of the frightful shock it was to her husband when she confessed the matter to him. He spoke of persuading the man not to take action against me for alienation of affection."

"Two years after!" Paula put in.

"Well, exactly. His suggestion was that I make a handsome allowance for the child, in which case she will drop all charges."

"Which you wouldn't, Steve!"

"My dear, to pay her as much as five cents on such a claim would be to put my head in a noose for life."

"Well, I should hope so!" Paula sat back, breathing again.

"And now what happens?" Deborah asked.

"Nothing. He's out of pocket the gas he used between here and San Francisco, and he writes her or sees her—I believe he has an office in Los Angeles—and tells her we won't fight. Only," Stephen finished, smiling, "with this senator talk coming up—it would be a nice time for an illegitimate child to appear in the picture!"

"Horrors!" Paula murmured, alarmed again.

"What on earth has been going on, and who was the murderer who was out on the lawn?" Marlys asked, coming in. But she waited for no answer. "Mother, Di telephoned," she said, "and they're all going to the movies tonight. How about me?"

"Darling, you were up late last night——" Paula was beginning. But Marlys cut across her.

"But we're going to the seven show, Mother, and then to Di's for just sandwiches and things—she said not even cake, and we're going to break up at ten-thirty. Please, Mother!"

"If you say ten-thirty and you *mean* ten-thirty," Stephen said.

"Honest to goodness, Dad!"

He laughed.

"I can trust you, I guess. Who's going? Need movie money?"

"I have money, Dad. I'm stopping for Jean and to get some celestials."

"Some what?"

"Celestials. Those big sugary cookies that they make at the Swan. The boys love them. Ken Briggs simply— breathes them in!" Marlys laughed joyfully, and they all laughed; it was so good to have her on her feet, young and gay again. The cloud passed from Paula's spirit; the Porcher episode had been no more than a bad dream. But it was funny to have Stephen take it so seriously, put her on the witness stand as it were.

She went into the nursery, where Mimsie was smearing herself with Pablum under Fanny's careful middle-aged eye. Marlys had been called to the telephone, Fanny explained, and had hurled the baby into her care. Paula smiled, shaking her head. Marlys had been out of her wits since last night's dissipation. She settled down next to the high chair, took over responsibility for little Mimsie's finishing of her supper, her transfer into woolly pajamas, her settlement in bed.

"Thanks, Fanny. I'll manage now. I may take her into my room for a while; the judge loves to have her to play with just before she goes to bed."

"Mom-mom-momom-mom!" Mimsie said.

"Yes, but you eat your Pablum now like a good girl. Not all over your bib, darling! The audacity of that woman!" Paula thought. "The brazen boldness of her! Sending a shyster like that Porcher in to bother Steve. Well, I'm not going to think about it!" And then, in a moment, "But I wish to goodness people were decenter and had to tell the truth, and then things like this couldn't happen! If ever there were any publicity about it, some of it would cling to Steve, and it's just not fair! Why, according to that, anybody could say anything about anybody—anything at all—and needn't have any proof, but the scandal would stick! She could be sued,

I know she could, and if we hear another word about it I'm going to make Steve sue her! But I wish to *goodness* it hadn't happened!"

Deborah had meanwhile gone into Marlys' room to watch her change her dress and discuss the plan for the evening.

"It's not a party," Marlys said; "just that we were all saying last night that we'd like to see this show, and Di said that if her mother would let her we could go to her house afterward."

"I think that's terribly nice of Mrs. Briggs. It means she gets home from the library and goes right at making sandwiches."

"Oh, she loves it, Aunt Deb!"

"She loves Diana and Ken. She was such a pretty girl, too, and now she always looks so tired. She was a senior at high when I went in, and I used to admire her so. Is Condy going tonight, Marlys?"

"Well, he's asked," Marlys said, all interest. "Di asked him by telephone before they all started for town this morning. But he said if he and the Arnolds—leave it to them to carry him off to town today!—he said that if he couldn't make the movie he'd at least try to come to Di's afterward. But I don't suppose he will."

"Why, why not? I should think the Arnold girls would."

"They'll probably ask him to their house to supper and go to a later show," Marlys predicted gloomily.

"Well, if he does come, remember that the more attractive the other boys think you, the more attractive he will," Deborah advised. "Don't pay any particular attention to him, but pick out someone like Roger Messenger—I suppose he'll be there. Doesn't he board with the Briggses?"

"He has a room there. I think he hashes for his meals most of the time. Oh, he'll be there," Marlys said, "smelling of the laboratory, with his hands all sweaty."

"What a horrible way to talk about a nice boy!"

"Well, he's only a boy," Marlys said slightingly. "He's twenty-two, just in medical school, and I always imagine him cutting up cold dead frogs or dusting off skulls all day! However, I'll be nice to him."

"Only don't keep watching Condy, and listening to him, and waiting to have him notice you—"

"Oh, Aunt Deb, I have sense!"

Her aunt kissed her, laughing, at the door.

"Well, have you?" But Marlys, as she ran toward the garage and jumped into the little blue car that since her eighteenth birthday had been the pride of her life, knew that Aunt Deb was as keen as she was that she should have a good time.

It began dully enough. Jean was full of spirit when Marlys stopped at the Forsyth house to pick her up, and Di was deeply grateful for the cookies, as was Di's mother, already busy in the kitchen. But there were no boys. Ken Briggs was going to join them when he could; Roger Messenger never got home until after seven. Still another unescorted girl, Vera Houston, arrived and announced that her brother Ollie was coming and going to bring Paul Shroeder, and Betty-Lou Barstow was waiting for them at the ticket office of the movie house. But still it was only girls!

"Should we get tickets and try to hold seats?" Betty-Lou asked. It all seemed rather drab and flat in the six-o'clock afternoon light. Going to the movie in daytime with no boys——

However, Ollie and Paul actually joined them before they had bought their seats, and decided against any attempt to hold seats for the others. They might not come at all. Probably wouldn't, after a day in town.

So they went in and were presently absorbed in the film. And sure enough, within fifteen minutes Jim

Lane and Condy and the Arnold girls were rustling and whispering in behind them, giggling over the muttered protests of neighbors and, for Marlys at least, making the occasion suddenly complete and thrilling.

When they came out, a little dazed and jaded, at twenty minutes past eight, Marlys could accommodate three beside herself in her car, and Condy was not among the three. She had a horrible suspicion, as he went off in the Barstow car, that he might not be coming to Di's; he might be going off to do something fascinating elsewhere, where there were lights and awnings and green cotton vine leaves on white trellises.

But he did come to Di's, and in no time at all everything there was wild gaiety and confusion and racket and delight. The girls gathered in the little bedroom Di shared with her mother and a sewing machine and an old-fashioned carved-walnut double bed. Here they powdered their noses and fluffed their curls before rushing out to see what they could do to help Mrs. Briggs. But everything was ready: all nicely arranged were paper napkins and paper plates, towers of sandwiches, and a pot of coffee that smelled too delicious. Two fancy cake plates, decorated with painted plums and grapes, held the big, frail, toothsome celestials.

Everything in Di's house said "poverty," loud and clear. But that did not matter; the crowd always had a glorious time when it was there. The parlor connected with a back parlor which was Ken's bedroom, so the folding doors were always closed; the gas stove in the kitchen had had thirty years of hard wear; the rooms were lighted by single unhooded bulbs that hung starkly from the center of the ceilings. One of the parlor's chief ornaments was a crayon portrait from a photograph of the late Kenwood Briggs, D.D.S., which stood on a gilded easel embellished by a sheaf of wheat tied with purple chenille.

The entertainment went with a glorious rush. No time to think whether one was popular or not, for everyone was talking and laughing and joking at once, and there were plenty of boys: Jim and Ken and Roger, Ollie Houston and Paul Shroeder, and the girls rushing about with cups and plates were kept in spasms of mirth. Mrs. Briggs, her office dress protected by a ruffled apron that Marlys had given her on her birthday, did not so much preside as keep the whole thing moving; here was mustard and here was sugar, and if the boys would sit on the floor—Ken, get the couch cushions—

Her sandwiches were famous. She had ingenious

ways of combining crab with mayonnaise and lettuce, and cream cheese with peanut butter and jelly, and brown bread and white bread and rye bread, that made just sandwiches seem like a very varied meal, and for Carol, who could not drink coffee, she had a cup of hot chocolate, and for Roger, who had had a long day in the laboratory, a special sandwich of bacon and eggs.

And with it all she kept them talking so comfortably, and entering in upon absurd games so spontaneously, that the feast might have been much simpler than it was and the house much smaller and hotter—though that hardly seemed possible—without dampening the spirits of the company at all.

They played Geography and Who Am I? while they ate, and Categories. Condy had never played these games; he seized upon them with the childlike ardor of one who had missed them as a child. "Demmit, you people have fun!" he said.

When it came Marlys' turn to propose a category she stated frankly that she had thought one up during her weeks in the hospital and that she was going to Honolulu and taking with her a ball and a racket.

A golf stick and a croquet mallet having quickly disposed of the obvious solution, there was a pause. Silence fell while they racked their brains to find the classification that might hold these two. Could Jean take a cup? No. A bowl? Yes. Vera could take a bowl.

There was great excitement. Vera had it!

"No, I haven't!" Vera lamented. "I don't know why I said that. It was just guesswork."

"Guess again, Vera!" Condy said feverishly. "What do we know of this girl?" he presently demanded. "Is she to be trusted? Is she bright?"

Oh, joy, joy, joy, it was all such fun! Members of the group stared severely at Marlys, as if to read her thoughts. Others dropped their faces against their pressing fingers and murmured distractedly, "I can take a bowl, a boil, a racket. I can take a fish and a flounder but not a whale."

"Yes, you can take a whale," Marlys said, "but not a shark."

"If I were Shakespeare could I take a shark?" Roger Messenger said. Marlys looked at him doubtfully.

"You're so smart, Roger," she said, "that I haven't any doubt you could. But I don't think so."

"Come on out in the hall," Roger said. Marlys went out with him and put her curls and her curled pink ear close to his mouth as he whispered, "Don't you remember something is 'sharked up' in *Hamlet?*"

"No, I don't. But that's right, anyway. It's a word that's a noun and a verb too."

"And a darned good category!" he said approvingly. "Say, did you have to be home at half-past ten?"

"Yes, but——"

"It's ten twenty-five." Roger hauled out a heavy old gold watch.

"Oh, it can't be!" She went back to the crowd disconsolate. "I have to go, Di. They're still treating me as if I was an invalid!"

"I'm not an invalid," Carol said briskly, "but we were up all night and in town all today, and my mother will raise the roof if we aren't home early."

"I wasn't in town today," Condy said. "I was up at coll, trying to get my credits fixed. But after all, I did fly out from New York only yesterday, and I could do with some sleep."

"Weren't you in town, Condy?" Marlys Hazeltine raised innocent eyes to his; she was standing, small and flushed and breathless from laughing, close beside him.

"I went up with the Arnolds first, but I came right down again." Somehow this information pleased her immensely. He had been having just the usual dull day of college registration, not doing mysterious and delightful things with the Arnolds.

"Will you drop us on your way home, Marlys?" Vera asked.

"I don't like Marlys to drive those three blocks further alone," Mrs. Briggs put in concernedly.

"I'm going back for a couple of hours' work," Roger said. "If Marlys will take me as far as her house, then it's only half a mile further."

So it was settled that way. If Marlys had dreamed of Condy going home with her and perhaps coming in to meet her father and mother, the dream died unborn. But no matter, the evening had been a glorious success, and Condy had shown himself as enthusiastic about the silly games and the general nonsense as was the least sophisticated among them. Marlys was hardly conscious of the Houstons' good nights, when Roger stopped the car for them at their gate, or of anything Roger happened to say afterward. He left her at her own door, took the car around to the garage; there was a flare of light out there for a minute or two, then the motor engine suddenly stopped and the light faded; everything was darkness.

Marlys went in, saw a light in the library, and peeped in. Her father and Senator Saintsbury were talking. "You're a fool if you don't, Steve," she heard the visitor say. Her father held out a hand to her, smiling.

"Come give me a kiss, pussy," he said. "Tired?"

"Oh no, I could have stayed all night!" Marlys gave her hand to old Philip Saintsbury, kissed her father, went yawning upstairs. But when she got into bed it was again to lie awake, lost in radiant, wide-eyed dreams.

Silvery rain had been falling at intervals all day and all night. Now, when it was slitting brightly through the March sunshine, Deborah Trezavant came out into it boldly, ready for a walk. She did not too often have time for walks, and of all weathers this was the sort that tempted her most. Soft air, blooming gardens, earth sending forth a very richness of scent, purple clouds rolling across the struggling sunshine. Wind was whipping idly about the corners here and there and bending the young birches and the tasseled peppers; Deborah took off her hat and let it ruffle her tawny hair as she followed the street up to its abrupt ending against the Barkers' gate and turned southwest upon an earthy lane. The town straggled into orchards and old gardens here, with the cupolas and gables of an earlier day peering through the trees. Oaks had once had these rolling hills to themselves, but three generations ago peppers and eucalyptus had been planted, poplars and palms. The damp leaves of the lane were covered with the tiny gold feathers of acacia and the deep pink of clustered pepper berries, and in the old gardens pampas grass and syringa were heavy and bowed with diamonds. There was a smell of age everywhere: old moldy bricks and mossy paths, old evergreen hedges with jeweled webs spread upon them, greenhouses sunk in earth, the paint scraped from their glass sides, panes broken, flowerpots tumbled and half buried in sod.

Deborah mounted upward through a series of rambling paths to a little dip on the edge of the woods where stood a brick house almost concealed by its overshadowing oaks and its overgrown garden. It was a small house of a story and a half, with windows flanking an unpretentious doorway and two prim dormers looking down upon a jungle of bushes and weeds. Plumbago, marigolds, periwinkle, alyssum, everything that could run wild had flourished here; a suffocated lemon verbena tree was draped with a red rambler rose; ivy had mounted into the oaks and hung from them in festoons.

The paneled white doorway was closed and locked; the window shades were drawn. But Deb followed a broken brick path about the house to the back and stood for a long minute looking about her.

Sunshine was streaming down against a light, half-hearted mist of rain. It lighted a row of barns and sheds, set against the edge of the woods, and blazed in blossoming plum and apple trees. Fences and paddocks were irradiated; the deep sweet green of the new grass that was deep all about them, the brightness of the light, and the ominous darkness of a great purple cloud hanging close above gave a dramatic value to the homely farm scene that all but took Deborah's breath.

She turned back to the house; a wing had been thrown out to the southwest, a pleasant long, low, brick room with one lofty north window, against whose outer sill Deborah could lean while she looked long and steadily within.

It was a shabby room, showing every sign of long years of vacancy and neglect. There were books here and there on the shelves that lined the walls; a few were scattered on the long worktable that occupied the center of the floor space. The big main rug had been rolled up at the ends and lay in two heaps on the floor. Several lamps had been huddled into a corner; there was no screen in the great fireplace; logs were still piled beside it; fine dust and ash had settled upon every surface in the place. On the table was a tray, powdered deep with its own share of dust, bearing three pink cups and a teapot. Here and there manuscript papers had drifted from the neighborhood of an uncovered typewriter that stood near the tray.

After her deliberate scrutiny Deborah sighed, straightened herself, and looked about at the orchard and barns and sky as if reorienting herself in a world from which she had for a while escaped. The rain had stopped now; a yellow sunset was piercing the clouds over the low line of hills toward the west. The college chimes sounded five slow strokes. She must start for home if she was to be in time for Mimsie's supper hour, an event which both Mimsie and her aunt regarded as one of the highlights of the day.

She walked about the house to the front garden again, stopped short, her heart beating a little fast. There was nothing of which to be afraid; it was broad daylight, the nearest farm was but a three minutes' walk away, and if she enjoyed wandering about the old place so might someone else. Nevertheless the sound of a step on the bricks out of sight frightened her. The quicker she turned the corner of the house and met whoever it was, the less nervous apprehension need she endure.

Instinctively sensing this, she moved faster and came in sight of the front garden in time to see a tall man, thin and stooped, with a shock of thick gray hair uncovered, turn toward the gate. His back was toward her, but even from that she knew she had nothing to fear; this was no marauder, no prowler. The hand that rested on a stick was gloved; the caped raincoat, though evidently long worn, spoke somehow of a personality. An old man looking at the house? "Oh, don't let him buy it, don't let him buy it!" she said to some powers unspecified in her heart.

He turned, hearing the scrape of her foot on the brick walk, and their eyes met. For a second complete stupefaction held Deborah dumb, then she went toward him.

"Barry! Barry Washburn!"

He was wearing dark glasses against the glare of the too-brilliant day; he took these off and returned her smile as he took her hand.

"Well, well, well! D'you know I was thinking of you

—only yesterday," he said with pleasant, unemotional cordiality. "I asked Bert de la Tour about you."

"But, Barry, how long have you been here?" she stammered.

"I arrived in San Francisco—let me see—this is Friday. I got in Wednesday after rather a rough flight," he said. "I came down to the campus last night, ran into De la Tour, and of course nothing would satisfy the dear fellow but he must put me up. I told his wife she wouldn't want a cranky old professor for a guest, but she appears to be as hospitable as he is."

So friendly, impersonal, pleased! Deborah felt ice forming about her heart; her throat was thick and dry. She must get her bearings—she musn't betray herself——

"And you came up to have a look at the old place?"

"I came out to walk. I was feeling pretty stuffy after three days in New York and the trip. And I somehow turned this way. It looks as if Nature was rapidly reclaiming her own," Barry Washburn said. "Of course," he added as they walked together down the lane, back toward the town, "you *can* walk in New York, and some men I know there actually do. But the distances are pretty great, and this time I had a good deal to do. But

Findlay, now," he added comfortably, "I had my first instructorship under John Findlay, and by George!" the man went on, interrupting himself to laugh, "that man walked miles—eighteen, twenty. Used to walk around the city sometimes on Sunday; start at the college, go down the west side to Bowling Green, and come up through the Ghetto and the park to the college again! Phenomenal. His family left him in Vermont one summer and came down to open the city house, and old John walked home! Well, how's the world going with Miss Trezavant?"

"Finely," Deborah answered with outward composure. He looked down at her sideways. She wore an old pleated plaid skirt, a soft roll-neck white sweater; her blue-checked raincoat swung open; her tawny hair was blown and uncovered.

"You look it!" he said. "I knew you instantly. But I am surprised that you recognized me. My mirror shows me a pretty old man these days. By the way, it *is* still Miss Trezavant?"

"Still Miss Trezavant. Changes don't come as rapidly to Ravenshill as they do other places. I am Emily Brontë *redivivus*," Deborah said; "only instead of Emily's dogs I have Paula's children—four of them."

"Four? There was a small girl, I know—seven or eight, was she? And two boys?"

"And now another girl, 'for dessert,' Stephen says. And all the babies of the Home," Deborah added. "I manage the Children's Hospital."

"And books. Still the old biographies?"

The earth shook beneath her. They had prowled through old bookstores in San Francisco on a rainy, shining afternoon like this eleven years ago. Barry had been hunting something about the Antarctic. Undersea growths? Algae, had it been?

"Still the old biographies. And how are the deep-sea fauna?"

"Why, I've got approximately seventy-five thousand references ready for classification on them," Professor Washburn said in his pleasant, academic voice. "I'm planning to do that before summer sessions begin. Then I'm to give two courses here."

"At Ravenshill?"

"That's what's under discussion now."

"How nice!" If he could be so removed, so smugly serene, she could attempt a poor imitation of it too. "Shall you take possession of the old place, do you think?"

"I hardly think so. I may stay at the club in San Francisco for a while. It's not worth while to clean the place up for five or six months. It would take weeks to begin with. And in September I may be going South."

"Los Angeles?"

"No, down into that ice belt, probably. Larkin may go. That's all on the knees of the gods."

"You used to talk of south Georgia."

"South Georgia, that's it exactly! Larkin can't finance an expedition, but he's trying to make some deal with the whaling boats."

"But, Barry, they go in for six months, don't they?"

"I wish half my students had your memory," he said. "You're absolutely right, but I don't suppose you've given it a thought since I picked up that old book years ago. Yes, they go in for a long season. However, nothing's definite about that. And here we are at the Hazeltine gate. Will you remember me most cordially to all of them—little Marlys, too, and your sister?"

"But surely you'll come in and see them all for yourself? It's just a family dinner tonight."

"I wish I could. But unfortunately Dr. Swedenborg is coming to the De la Tours tonight, and I've got to straighten out my schedule with him. But I'll see you all very soon if you'll give me a rain check on that very kind invitation."

She watched him walk down the street, the rain whirling his cape over his head, whirling it away again to show the thick gray hair, the slightly stooped shoulders. Then she went into the house and shut the door.

There was an armchair with a high leather back in the hall; Deborah walked toward it and sat down, staring ahead of her. A clock ticked steadily somewhere, and over a hundred tiny, indistinguishable sounds she could hear Fanny scolding away steadily in the pantry. A bright triangle of last sunlight faded suddenly from the turn of the stairway and the rain began again, tapping and rustling. Cars honked far away; a door somewhere slammed. Paula's voice came laughingly from upstairs, out of sight.

"Mimsie, come back here with that! Come back, you scamp! Teevy, grab her!"

Then a hoarse laugh from Teevy and a crescendo of ripples of baby mirth from Mimsie—squeals, whimpers, the laughter that is all ready to turn into tears. Feet stamped in the upper hall. Paula called:

"See if Aunt Deb's in her room, Teevy. If she's not lying down, tell her to come in and see Mrs. Broome!"

No, Deb would not see Mrs. Broome. Smartly groomed, crimped, creamed, curled, rouged Mrs. Broome, who had been in school with Paula and was now complacently displaying a third husband, like a battle trophy. Deborah went quietly through the dining room, quietly up a flight of back stairs, up another flight, high up to the top rooms where the boys lived and where there was a deserted study. Here she had often come to read as a little girl, to dream as an older girl; no one would find her here.

There was an old couch in a corner. Deborah flung aside her raincoat and rubbers, piled pillows on the couch, and lay down, her locked hands behind her, her eyes fixed absently on space. Against the room's two dormer windows rain was slatting; the windows were dusty, and the rain made runnels in the dust. There was a soothing sound of pattering on the roof; now and then a breeze rippled over the world and the young leaves in the garden rustled. The air in the study was chill and stale and scented with vague aromas of leather and wood and mice.

Chapter Four

DEBORAH PULLED an old comforter over her feet; the hard, puzzled look on her face did not change. Daylight died at the windows; the world outside was all dripping dusk. Stephen's car buzzed in the garage, was still; Deb could hear him shouting some message to Trez.

A typical professor, gray and cheerful and pleasantly dry in manner; in all the eleven years when she had thought of him, thought of him every day, perhaps every hour, she had never imagined him so! He had always been to her the man she had met at Daisy Pope's tea—the tall, dark, serious newcomer who was to give six lectures at Ravenshill. She had been twenty-five then, all rapture over the unique experience of meeting a man who loved as much as she to talk books; his lectures had been on modern poets, and she had attended them all. They had walked down Maiden Lane from the lecture room, still talking, and sometimes he had come in to the Trezavant house, and when he did Wong Foo had always had tea waiting. If it were magical summer weather—and all that summer seemed in retrospect to be one golden dream of shady, fragrant afternoons—they moved to the table out on the lawn. Old Dr. Trezavant had been living then. His daughters had seen that he had a cup of tea at four o'clock; there had been no disruption of the family order to include a guest at the festive little meal.

Sometimes Paula had come over with fairylike Marlys dancing beside her, little Teevy marching gallantly, Trez in the pushcart. Then there were always cookies for the children and a dog biscuit for T'narly. Beautiful, champagne-colored old T'narly, who lay beside the baby's cart and growled at strangers.

Conversation would be general then until Paula went

away and the old doctor left them to wander through his orchid conservatory or retire to the library for a nap before dinner. And when they were alone Deborah and Barry could return to the talk that seemed all of poetry and yet that grew to be more and more of themselves.

Francis Thompson and Alice Meynell, Housman and Whitman, Emily Dickinson and always Shakespeare, these had been her guides to a world of enchantment that made the everyday world seem further and further away, dimmer and dimmer to her senses. She had been conscious only that at the Varsity Arms there was living a tall, dark, handsome man whose lightest word was witchery to her, whose briefest glance was enough to send her floating off, floating away from reality, no solid ground beneath her feet, just waves—waves—waves of sheer ecstasy and agony washing over her.

Merely to meet a neighbor, to hear the casual, pleasant query, "Aren't the Washburn lectures simply marvelous, Deborah?" had filled her with mysterious delight and pain. Half the women in town had been in love with him. "He ought to be playing Romeo somewhere," Amy Chouteau had said. "He's fascinating, simply fascinating," Paula had conceded. Deborah had been conscious of a fierce, unreasoning jealousy of their admiration; they ought not to admire him; she would have been happier to be the only one who appreciated his dark, stern, quiet charm.

She had been motherless since childhood; it was strange to her to hear that he had been motherless, too, since small-boy days. A family friend, unrelated, "Aunt Rose," had been his mother—rich, widowed, passionately devoted to him. She had lived for him, taken him abroad after college, encouraged him; he had said that someday his book would be dedicated to "Aunt Rose."

"She never had children of her own?" Deborah had asked.

"A daughter. Marcia. Delicate." He had frowned as if the thought of Marcia had disturbed him. "Something went wrong," he had said, hesitating for words. "Marcia's all there—not insane, not feeble-minded. In fact, in lots of ways she's very strong-minded. But not quite right. Vague. She'll stay for days in her room, silent, and then suddenly come out as gay as a lark, wanting to dance. It's been a terrible grief for Aunt Rose. Marcia has her own suite of rooms, her own maid—a sort of companion maid. Sometimes she'll work in the garden, get herself all warmed up and tired, and then she's like any other girl. And you should see my aunt's face then!

But then a day or two later Marcia'll get serious—we all know it's coming on——"

"You said 'a girl,' Barry?"

"Not now, really. Marcia's two years older than I am. Thirty-eight."

"And you three live together?"

"In my aunt's old house in Milton, yes."

"That's probably," the radiant girl who had been Deborah Trezavant had said speculatively, "why you haven't married. You've been repaying your aunt by being there with her, helping with Marcia."

She remembered saying it; she remembered a fine-striped dimity frock with a full skirt and a great pink rose at the belt. She remembered the grape arbor of Dave Bartlett's house on a hot summer afternoon: sunlight piercing the green leaves and touching the hard green beads of the growing grapes. The man had laughed and flushed uncomfortably.

"There's no repaying Aunt Rose. She's—royal. She took charge of a lonely kid of six with one great sweep. Certainly I could have a bicycle, and certainly someday I could have a gun, and of course we kids could have the big basement room for a club. Whatever came along was mine by right; of course she and I and Marcia were going to the circus—of course I could build an airplane! The atmosphere of the world changed for me, opened up. Marcia was quite normal then. Those were happy times."

Looking at him thoughtfully, Deborah had speculated as to what had changed those happy times. Something had. His face had grave lines now; it was not natural that a man like Barry, loved by all women, should have come to his age unwed.

She had not been long in coming to the conclusion that the answer was Marcia. Every innocent allusion he made to his foster sister confirmed the conviction. Marcia loved walking, "if she can get someone to walk with her." Marcia loved music. "We go to all the symphonies and concerts," Barry had said, "and she's at her best in the box, with the house darkened, listening to music."

"She's in love with you, Barry, isn't she?" Deborah had dared ask.

"I suppose so," he had answered unsmilingly after a moment. "She would fall in love with any man who was as much with her as I am. She has that—that quality of interpreting—interpreting friendship that way. It's half imagination, with Marcia. When she was younger she would tell me that this boy or that boy had written her a letter or said something quite unmistakable. It used to worry Aunt Rose. She knew it was Marcia's wishing—imagining—"

And he had stopped, distressed, unwilling to be quite frank about it. But Deborah had known what he was trying to say. Every group of girls, every boarding school, has its Marcia. The girl who invents the romances that do not come to her, the girl whose life is one long flattering dream.

The summer, and the Washburn lectures, had come to an end. Barry had set his date of departure; he must be in Chicago in mid-September. Deb had not dreaded the parting, because it would have been easier to think of her life deprived of her own brain, her own entity and consciousness, as to imagine it without Barry. He was as much a part of her now as a sixth sense. His voice was perpetually in her ears; the touch of his hand was warm on her own. The chairs in which he had sat, the lawns across which they had so often strolled, the college with its Spanish-tiled low roofs and blue-shadowed arcades and cloisters were all a part of it. Deborah could be hungry, thirsty, perhaps cold; but she could never again be without the very essence of her life and being, and that was Barry.

He was to go away in the early morning. Deborah would be at the station to say good-by. Their last evening together would be their only chance for privacy or confidences.

They had spent it walking about the college grounds and the low rolling hills, under a white full moon. The world had been enchanted that night; nothing had seemed real. Not the oaks, and the lacy black shadows under them, and the silver-washed roofs, and the dim, furry, faraway hills.

They had leaned on a fence, looking down at the town, and Barry had said, suddenly and gruffly:

"There's something I want to say to you."

Deborah's voice had shaken between laughter and tears; she had held it low.

"Well, I should h-h-hope so!"

"I've nothing in the world to offer you," he had said. "I'm eleven years older than you are. You're rich and you're beautiful—you've everything! But I can't go away not telling you—I'd be crazy to go away not telling you. I'm not made of cold steel. I could have been as gay, as good at games, as your brother and sister and all of you," he had stumbled on, painfully, pitifully, and her heart had been wrung for him. "But my life hasn't been

—that way. I've got to go back now to a house with no laughter in it—no lightness. No picnicking up on Deer Ridge and having you start a fire. No days on the beach at Halfmoon Bay—nothing, nothing like that. Wouldn't I be a fool," he had rushed on fiercely, "if I hadn't come to love you! Wouldn't I be a fool if all this sunshine, this friendliness, these talks and walks—all the laughter—Marlys calling me 'Uncle Barry,' Paula asking me to hold Trez for a few minutes—— What have I ever had in my life like that? School, concerts, with Aunt Rose and Marcia. Europe, the best rooms everywhere, the finest opera tickets—with Aunt Rose and Marcia. I love them, they're mine, I have to keep them happy—but I've lived out here, Deb," he had added, suddenly broken. "I've been alive. I've breathed it in and filled my lungs and my soul and my heart—and I want you to know that no man ever worshiped a woman as I worship you. Just your hand——" He had had it at his lips. "Just—— My God, if it could be mine! If you'd wait! If you'd let me think that somewhere in your heart you've got a little place for me!"

She had not had to answer in words. She had turned, putting one arm about his neck, and then the madness of their first long kiss had been on them, and the deep waters had swept them away, and the stars had reeled in the warm, low summer sky.

And after that dizzying, breathless embrace they had faced each other in the white moonlight, laughing, their cheeks wet, and so had gone to talk, the first wonderful talk of when and when and when, and then his lips had been against hers again and his arms crushing the breath out of her body.

"Barry, with me it was from the first instant. See how shameless I am. Say that it was from the first instant with you too."

"But I can't, my darling. Because I never dreamed a dry Boston professor—because all this seemed like too bright a thing to be real—California and the pepper trees and the fogs coming over the range, and your sister's house full of babies and sunshine, and tea in the garden with you coming out in a blue dress with a puppy in your hands——"

"The brown puppy!"

"It all seemed like something too exquisite—too ideal to be true, Deb. And then when you came flashing back at me with Vachel Lindsay and Millay and Pompilia——"

"And 'daffodils,' " she had said, " 'that come before the

swallow dares, and take the winds of March with beauty!'"

"But it doesn't matter now!" he had rejoiced, under that long-ago summer moon.

"Only—you must go back, Barry?" This had been later, when they had somewhat come to their senses and were walking home.

"I must go back. To tell them—to tell Aunt Rose. And then I'll come West again. Not to go back any more."

"But how terribly lonely they'll be, alone in that big Milton house," she had presently said.

"I know. I think of that. But why wouldn't it be possible, Deb, for them to come away too? To some little warm place at Carmel, perhaps, or in the Los Altos hills. Some place where old Maria and perhaps a cook would be all they'd need, and life would be so much simpler."

"Oh, if they would! I'll live for that. And letters——"

But there had been only two letters. One from the train. A long silence, and then the second. Barry had written that his aunt was dead and that he had been married that day to Marcia. That was all.

That was all, until today. And today's meeting had accentuated the sense of pain and loss in Deb's heart until she felt that she could hardly bear it.

It was dark now in the upstairs study. She sat up on the couch, feeling fuzzy and stupid, got to her feet, descended to her own room, and looked at herself in her dressing-table mirror.

"A fussy-looking middle-aged woman," she said half aloud.

However, when the rich, soft, tawny hair was brushed and braided and her face freshened and a touch of red put on her mouth, the outlook was more cheering, and Paula, coming in to watch her sister dress and to gossip, could quite truthfully say, "Deb, you're beautiful."

Deborah looked without enthusiasm at the clean pure tan of her skin, the feathery black eyebrows over widely spaced blue eyes, the broad mouth, and said firmly, "Never."

"Well, you're the only person who doesn't think so," Paula said. And then, with sudden interest, "Deb, you met Barry Washburn?"

"Who said so?" Deb asked, taken by surprise.

"I met him. Daisy Pope and I were up on the campus taking up some card tables for tomorrow night and we saw him. He came over to the car and told us he'd seen you walking. Deb, isn't he the most changed human being you ever saw? Why, he looks sixty! And he can't be—— How old is he?"

"About forty-six or seven, I should think."

"Well, I hardly knew him. I honestly don't think I would have known him. But Daisy saw them in Boston about two years ago, so she recognized him. I asked him to dinner Sunday night. I'm going to get someone to help Fanny. The Saintsburys and the Popes and Prent, of course, and the three of us. That's only eight. Marlys has a date with the Arnolds. Deb, didn't you think he was terribly changed?"

"The gray hair—I somehow hadn't thought his hair would go gray. I've acquired some," Deb said, looking at herself in the mirror, "but it surprised me to see that he had."

"Gray hair, and that stoop! Oh dear, dear," Paula said, "and he used to be our Adonis! I can remember thinking he was like every book hero I'd ever loved— Byron and Copperfield and the Virginian and Sherlock Holmes! How'd you happen to meet him?"

"I was walking in the rain up near the old Bartlett place and I saw him in the garden."

"That place is his now, isn't it?"

"Yes. Dave Bartlett left it to him, but I don't believe

he's seen it—in fact, I know he hasn't—in all these years. But when Barry was here he and I and Dave used to have wonderful evenings there, and now and then I walk in and have a look around. It's in bad repair now."

"Is he going to live there?"

"He said not. He seemed to feel"—Deborah slipped a dress over her head—"he seemed to feel that it would be a good deal of bother. His plans are so uncertain. He's doing research on some Antarctic work now, and he lectures this summer at Ravenshill. But he seemed rather vague about it all."

"D'you suppose he got all his wife's money?"

"I never thought of it. But I don't see who else would get it."

"That would give him a free hand for all his explorings, of course. But I must say," Paula interpolated with a little deprecatory laugh, "his appearance doesn't suggest wealth. You hadn't known he was coming, had you, Deb?"

"I? Oh no."

"Was it a shock to you to see him?"

"Yes, I think it was. It—brought it home to me, somehow. The long years, and the dreams—I suppose I thought we could go back," Deborah said with some little difficulty, between pauses. "That he would be the same and that I would be. 'The wind from my lost country blows beside me,' as Mrs. Meynell says. But he isn't the same man, naturally, and I'm not the same woman. He didn't call me 'Deborah' or 'Deb'; it was 'Miss Trezavant.'"

"Daisy Pope says that what he went through with Marcia must have been something awful," Paula said, watching her sister closely as Deborah went about the room hanging things in the closet, straightening the dressing table. "She was just weak-witted and queer, you know, breaking out quite sensibly sometimes, Daisy said, and then going vague again. It seems she was jealous of every word he said and every look he gave anyone else, used to go sit in his classroom if he spoke of any particular student; she told Daisy that herself and laughed about it. When Barry'd go to the telephone she'd ask, 'Who was that? What did he want?' and when Daisy and Barry got talking about old days here before he was married, she got furious and told him to shut up about it, she didn't want to hear it, and she rushed upstairs. He went up and brought her down again, but you can imagine what a nice luncheon they had after that."

"When'd you hear all this?"

"Just this afternoon. And, my dear," Paula said, off at a tangent as she recalled the conversation, "Mollie Butler's having sixteen for supper Sunday night, and when Marlys asked Condy if she were asked he said, 'First on the list!'"

"If ever I saw a feather in a spring gale——" Deborah said smilingly.

"Marlys?" Paula laughed complacently. "She's out of her senses," she conceded. "I only hope," the mother said, a trace of anxiety coming into her voice, "that he likes her half as much as she likes him."

"Half as much won't do, Paula."

"No, I suppose not. But there's no reason why he shouldn't like her, Deb," Paula argued.

"Except that it doesn't go by reason and never will go by reason. But there's no question that he likes her and finds her perfectly fascinating," Deb conceded. "Only —he's twenty-eight and Marlys is eighteen, and it's highly possible that he thinks of her as too young to be taken seriously."

"She has to have her experiences like the rest of us!" Paula said, not quite happy about it. "If we go to Washington—and Steve talked of it this morning as if we might—it will get her away from all the crowd here and give her a chance to meet other men at any rate!"

"Senator Saintsbury has talked Steve over, then?"

"He thinks it's all important. It's my conviction," said Paula, "that that's the real reason they put off their sailing until after the primaries. Yes, I think Steve is beginning to get excited about it now. He feels it will be a fight and he rather likes the idea."

" 'Senator Hazeltine,' " Deborah said, trying the sound. "Isn't it funny how things come into your life? Condy Cheeseborough for Marlys, this prospect for you and Steve, all coming up only a week or two ago."

"And Barry back in your life," Paula ventured. Deb faintly shook her head.

"A complete stranger back in my life," she said. "I found myself making talk with him. . . . Also back in our lives," she added in a lighter tone, "the ubiquitous Mae Singer."

"Steve hasn't heard any more of that?" Paula asked, alarmed. "Not since that man Porcher was here two weeks ago?"

"Not that I know of. But Porcher's final shot to Steve was—what was it? 'You'll shortly hear from me again.' "

"Steve didn't pay the slightest attention. He doesn't think they'll make any more trouble."

"I don't either. But I was thinking how unexpected it all is—those four separate little events coming along."

"And possibly," Paula said as they went downstairs, "in a few more weeks they'll all have vanished in smoke. Our gray-headed Adonis may decide not to stay here; he said it was all most indefinite; Marlys may take a fancy to someone else; Mae Singer may sink into oblivion; and Steve may lose at the primaries!"

"If life ever went like that!" Deborah laughed. "Is the judge downstairs, Fanny?" she asked of the elderly, severe-looking maid when they reached the lower hall.

"No ma'am," Fanny said. "And there's a lady and a gentleman waiting for him."

"Who—at this hour? It's nearly six," Paula said. "The youngsters were coming for Marlys, but I thought not until later."

"It's that Mrs. Singer," Fanny volunteered scornfully. Paula's face clouded.

"For pity's sake!" She swept into the library, catching at Deb's hand and drawing her along with her. "How do you do, Mae?" she said icily to the woman who rose from a couch to greet her.

"How do, Mrs. Hazeltine," Jay Porcher, who was Mrs. Singer's companion, said from a chair by the hearth. He did not rise. Paula glanced at him, glanced at the woman again, freezing them both with a look of ineffable scorn, and sat down. Deb, half seated against the table edge, was conscious that her heart was beating uncomfortably fast.

"I believe I've only seen Miss Trezavant twice before, but I remember her perfectly," Mae Singer said in a soft, friendly, timid voice. "It was just after you came back from South America, before I had to go away from my dear little farm."

A slender woman in her early thirties, she was dressed in a conservative flowered navy gown, with a dark coat and a small dark hat. She wore cotton gloves, and her shoes and handbag showed signs of long wear.

"I loved that little farm; it was heaven—it was escape for me," she said with a glance that asked sympathy from them all. "But affairs in New York made it necessary. And the thing is now, they've taken the children away from me, and I didn't know anywhere else to go for help."

"Where've they taken them?" Deborah asked sharply.

"To the Home in San José. On a charge of unfit guardianship," Jay Porcher supplied. "Somebody made claims that Mrs. Singer was—what was it?" he asked his client, amused. "Drugs, I believe. Traffic in drugs."

"Which is so terrible!" Mae breathed. Her eyes were round and pale blue, her hair fluffed into puffs of brownish gold. Her skin was clear and colorless and her expression one of patient suffering.

"Well, if they're taking good care of them," Paula said, encouraged by Deborah's practical stand, "and if you want to get a job, why not leave the children there for a while?"

"Oh, but you know what my children are to me, Paula!" Mae said.

Paula felt a disagreeable prick of premonition. Mae had never called her by her name before. It had always been a most respectful "Mrs. Hazeltine." What accounted for the change and the insolent confidence that underran Mae's outwardly mild manner tonight?

"Yes, I know," she said without sympathy. "But there are times——"

"There are times when a man must face his responsibilities, Mrs. Hazeltine," Porcher put in significantly. "We want to make this as pleasant and simple as we can for all parties. But you're aware of the situation, and the question is, what's the best way to handle it?"

"Then I have nothing whatever to say to you," Paula

said, pale with anger and rising to her feet. "And I advise you not to bother Judge Hazeltine with what is—what *was*—merely a charity case of mine, as Mae well knows, and none of his business at all."

"Lady, lady dear!" Mae said in a shocked tone, "we mustn't talk like this! It's only—only, you see, that Claire-Elise is still a baby, and that means that for a year or two I'll have to have help. All I want is a little place—I'm afraid it would have to be in town this time—where I can have the children with me, near a good school. I know," she interrupted herself to say earnestly, "I know there's no defense for me. You were kind to me, and Stephen and I betrayed you. We lost our heads; can't you see how natural that was? I wouldn't harm him, I wouldn't have one breath of this reach the public for anything in the world! You befriended me——"

"Especially now it wouldn't be any too good," Jay Porcher interpolated, "when there's talk of his running against Fenelli for senator."

"Ah, *that's* it!" Deborah thought. "It's a political frame-up. They've got hold of this miserable creature and they're going to play her against Steve!"

"Wouldn't the best thing be for him to take care of us? Oh, not in luxury like this!" Mae said, indicating with a wave of her hand the handsome library in which they sat. "Just some simple little place where I could have my babies with me."

"I never heard such nonsense!" Paula ejaculated. "You must know that these men are just using you for a purpose, Mae. I found you in a filthy slum and I brought you and the children——"

"Pardon me," Jay Porcher said, "but the check that brought Mrs. Singer to California was signed by Judge Hazeltine. We have a photostatic copy of it."

"You have a—what?" Paula said, stupefied.

"A friend of mine got into trouble with a check once," Mae supplied innocently, "and she told me always to have copies made."

"I should suppose you'd realize, Mr. Porcher," Deborah said coldly, "that the very fact that Mrs. Singer had that copied would indicate that this is mere blackmail."

"No, no," he said tolerantly, "it's a very usual thing."

"Blackmail!" Mae echoed. "Oh no! A mother's desire to get her babies under her wing isn't blackmail. I have no feeling of revenge against Stephen Hazeltine! I was wrong, I was bad, I know that. I was a married woman and I allowed my feelings to lead me into what I knew was wrong. I'm a sinner, but I sinned for love!"

"I don't care to talk to you any more, Mae. The whole thing is too ridiculous!" Paula said. Hard spots of uncomfortable color stood in her cheeks; she was breathing fast. "There is no court in the world that would pay the slightest attention to anything you can possibly say against my husband," she went on warmly. "What I think of your—your utter ingratitude for what I tried to do for your children I'll not say because I know it wouldn't make the slightest impression on you! I did all I could for you, and now you come and try to destroy my family and my happiness."

"Oh, please, please!" Mae Singer said in a fluttered voice. "I didn't want to come! I felt terribly about coming. But you see the *Clarion* wants the children's story; they've offered me five hundred dollars for it, and I had to consult Mr. Porcher to see what I ought to do!"

"The *Clarion!* What on earth have they got to do with it?" Paula demanded.

"They heard of it and sent someone to interview Mrs. Singer in my office," Jay Porcher said. "Now, there's a quiet, simple way of handling this that won't harm anyone," he went on ingratiatingly. "Judge Hazeltine—we won't go into what he did in taking advantage of a woman who was placed, as it were, in his charge, under deep obligations to him, defenseless——"

"Placed in his charge!" whispered Paula, swallowing.

"Men are weak, and my client admits her own mistake and is heartily sorry for it," Jay Porcher continued. "We are willing to call the past the past. Why not? We all have to do that. Live and let live! No, it's to the future that this brave little woman must look now. Life has treated her cruelly; no question of that. But she wants to face the days to come bravely, with her children about her. And to do that she needs help. This is no blackmail case; she isn't making any charges. She simply asks a woman's sympathy for the child who is half sister to your own children."

"I haven't had my baby in my arms for ten long days!" Mae said, tears in her eyes. "It would kill me to have the whole thing in the *Clarion* right now when Stephen is going into politics, but my husband is dead—I went back to him and took care of him until he died, and I've nowhere else to turn."

"What goes on?" It was Stephen, broad and serene and reassuring in the doorway. Paula turned to him with a gasp of relief.

"I've tried writing you four times, Judge," Jay Porcher said, a first trace of ugliness in his tone, "and I got tired of it."

"Yes, I had your letters," Stephen said, undisturbed. "But there didn't seem to be any appropriate answer. What's all this about? Suppose you girls beat it," he said, smiling at Paula and Deborah, "and I'll join you upstairs in a few minutes." And as his wife and her sister thankfully fled the scene they heard him say firmly, "Porcher, I haven't much use for your sort of law. My wife did what she could for Mrs. Singer and evidently failed. It might save us all considerable time for me to tell you that there's nothing more for you or for her to get out of this family!"

But when he entered his own bedroom a few minutes later his wife saw with an instant pang of apprehension that he looked tired and puzzled.

"Steve," she said, "I'll never forgive myself for bringing that woman into our lives. You never would have heard of her except for me! Did you ever in your entire life hear such impudence! What does a man like Porcher think he can gain from this sort of thing?"

"He might gain my withdrawing from the senatorial race," Stephen said slowly, sitting down.

"Paula, if Mae Singer has the nerve——" This was

Deborah, at the open doorway. "Oh, I didn't know Steve had got rid of that precious pair," she apologized, retreating.

"That precious pair," Stephen said with a rueful smile, "may cook my political ambitions!"

"Oh no!" Deborah said, aghast.

"Might," the man said.

"But, Steve," his wife said agitatedly, "you won't be such a *fool* as to let anything Mae Singer chooses to say affect your running for the Senate! Why, according to that, anybody who wanted to ruin anyone else could cook up some story——"

She stopped, turned about on the dressing-table seat, her soft hair loosened on her shoulders. Her husband shook his head.

"Steve, aren't there libel laws?" Deborah asked.

"Certainly there are libel laws, and even though I could prove injury, I could only bring a civil suit for damages; in that case I could collect from the libeler the amount fixed by the court for personal injury, and Mae Singer hasn't a cent to her name."

"Isn't there some way to shut her up?" Paula asked.

"Not that I know of. Mae evidently is a seasoned old hand at this sort of thing," the man said; "that business of having a check photographed—no amateur at the game would think of that. She's a professional blackmailer, very probably."

"You don't think so!"

"Well, it looks like it. When I last saw her a couple of years ago," Stephen said, "I got the impression she had been drinking, perhaps taking drugs; she looked frowzy and pale, as I remember it."

"Certainly she did! And her house was a perfect pigpen!" Paula supplied.

"Exactly. Now she turns up, slim and nicely dressed, looking as if she never had touched alcohol in her life. It's probable," Stephen said from his armchair, in which he had seated himself with his head thrown back and his narrowed eyes on space, "it's highly possible that the Fenelli outfit has gotten hold of her, seen that she has the right clothes and a respectable address, and has framed up this story to keep me from running."

"Well, if things like that can go on, it actually makes you lose faith in human nature!" Paula said.

"I don't see how she can get very far with it, Sis," Deborah added thoughtfully.

"No, I don't either!" Stephen agreed in a lighter tone. "Porcher is in it for a fifty-fifty break, of course. But

Porcher is one of the Fenelli attorneys, which made me think there might be more in it than meets the eye. Exactly how they happened to get together is a mystery, but it's likely that someone who knew of our interest in her case, and knew that she'd been practically thrown out of various houses round here, may have told him to get in touch with her."

"I'm amazed that they'll put the slightest trust in her," Paula said indignantly. "That is," she added, "if they really believe her and aren't just framing the whole thing."

"Well, *we* trusted her," Stephen reminded her, smiling; "she has that simple, genuine, honest manner, and she has three children as weapons. And she knows how to use them!"

"What was that classic last observation?" Deb mused. " 'I'm a sinner, but I sinned for love'!"

"Oh, it makes you sick, the whole thing!" Paula exclaimed despairingly.

"Now you forget the whole thing, Mother," Stephen said comfortingly. "We'll probably hear no more of it. But the coincidence," he added, "of this coming up exactly at this moment is—rather surprising, that's all! Let's put the whole thing aside. I'll have a talk with

Prentiss about Porcher; we may be able to unearth something there. Hello, where's the debutante going tonight?"

"Just out with the gang," Marlys said, coming into the room. She wore last winter's dark red suit, for the spring night was cold, and last winter's scoop-brimmed red hat, but she was so radiant in youth and happiness and beauty that she looked newly arrayed.

"Now listen——" her mother began. And then pleadingly, "Remember your accident, darling, and do be careful!"

"There are only four of us, in Jim's car," Marlys said. "Jean and Jim, Condy and I. Everything will be decorum itself."

"And where are you going?"

"Well, we looked at the movies round here, and they're all lousy," Marlys said frankly. "So we're going down to San José, and we'll see something, have sandwiches at O'Brien's, and come home early."

She stood tipping forward on her toes and sinking back on her heels, gesticulating with both wide-open arms, too brimful of felicity to hold her young, thrilling body still.

"Here, come to earth, young lady!" her father said.

"I'm happy!" She whirled about, kissing them all good night, flashed away.

Jean Forsyth was on the front seat with Jim and Diana. Ken Briggs and Condy were on the back seat, and they wedged Marlys in between them. She settled down comfortably, instantly pulling off her soft glove and slipping her small warm hand into Condy's. She was deliciously conscious of his own hand's enclosing pressure as they talked. Jim twisted about so that he could see them in the soft warm gloom of the twilight.

"We thought San José, see?"

"There's nothing here we haven't seen," Di explained.

"Why *not* San José?" Marlys said. Any place was heaven under the circumstances.

"Your mother care?"

"With Ken and Di to chaperon us? You feel up to chaperoning me, don't you, Di?"

"I do not," Di said definitely. "We have to be home right after the movies, anyway. We promised."

"Oh, I do too!" Marlys said as they started.

"Unless you and I go somewhere to dance," Condy said.

"Where could we go?"

"Plenty of places."

"You mean all of us?"

"Well—whoever would. We could switch to Jud Carter's car, or I could pick up mine."

"I couldn't," Marlys said faintly. Ken was leaning forward talking to the others now, and she and Condy could murmur unheard. She took his hand and pressed it against her cold soft cheek.

"Cut that out," he said. "I told you last week that it's very silly for young girls like you to imagine they're in love."

But he smiled down at her, close against his arm, as he said it, and as a fan of light from a street lamp passed over them she saw the smile.

"I'm not imagining it," she said.

"Want to break your silly little heart?" the man asked.

Marlys smiled back at him bravely.

"I guess so."

"You'd feel rotten, you know, if I were drafted or something and had to go away."

"You won't be."

"Never can tell."

"Don't tease me, Condy." Both her hands were in his now; she leaned back in the shelter of the big arm that went about her; she had no further need of words.

Too soon they were in the busy town. Its main street was a long blaze of lights and its sidewalks swarming at half-past six. The half-dozen movie offerings were advertised by flaming stars and twisting serpents of brilliance. Ken solemnly collected everyone's money; there was a moment's delay at the box-office window.

Then they were all in the dark, comfortably ensconced in loge seats, with music stealing out of the blackness and the quivering bright story unfolding itself on the screen. And again Marlys was next to Condy, and again her hand was in his. This left Ken and Di, brother and sister, to pair off, for Jim and Jean had been practically engaged for months, but Marlys, if she gave the situation a thought at all, dismissed it impatiently. Ken and Di were devoted to each other and always had jokes and confidences to exchange, and she couldn't help it, anyway! To waste an evening on pleasant, unexciting Ken Briggs, and let Di have Condy, would have been too bitter!

As it was, the occasion was all bliss until after the late hilarious supper, when they had a curved alcove to themselves and could communicate with the Arnolds, Jud Carter, and Betty-Lou, and a quiet, appreciative second lieutenant in the adjoining alcove. It was only when they were almost home at half-past ten that a sudden chill came over Marlys' spirit.

Condy had been making her feel very much the beloved woman all through the movie and the supper party. In the darkness of the theater he had more than once stooped unobserved to kiss the top of her head. At the table he had had eyes and interest only for her, or at least so much for her that his attentions to the others acted more as a foil than a distraction.

And on the drive home once again she was snuggled close to him, and when the others talked they could slip in a few quick whispers entirely their own.

But in the doorway of the Hazeltine house, restoring her to her family, when they were quite alone, she said to him wistfully:

"Then we're not going on to dance?"

"Your people wouldn't let you," he answered unencouragingly.

"I could ask them, Condy!" Her piquant little upraised face was all eagerness. "The light's still going in Dad's room," she said.

"No," he said unsmilingly, looking down at her as he absently hooked and unhooked the furred collar of the red coat.

"But Jim said he and Jean and the Arnolds might go somewhere!"

"You're like a baby, aren't you?" he asked.

"No, I'm not a baby! But the time I'm with you, Condy," she whispered, "is the only time I'm living! Between times, I'm only remembering! Please, please let's go dancing, you and I. I'll make it all right with Mother."

"I thought this was only fooling between you and me—you such a kid——" Condy said somewhat incoherently. He put his arm tightly about her and kissed her. Not once, not tenderly, but hard and harshly and many times. "You—you asked for it!" he said breathlessly, steadying her on her feet again as she swayed dizzily and might have fallen. Marlys could not speak, but her eyes were stars. "Don't you see—don't you see, you little fool, that I—I'm human!" Condy said. And instantly she was in his arms again, her body crushed, her face crushed against his.

And this time, when she was free again, neither spoke. Condy stood back, his hands jammed in his pockets, his breath coming a little fast, his tumbled leonine head bare.

Marlys gave him one look, between laughter and tears; one gasping little laugh escaped her as she fled upstairs.

Chapter Five

PAULA HAZELTINE sat at her breakfast table in all the glory of a soft May morning and wished herself a thousand miles away—anywhere, anywhere but here at home in Ravenshill, and in any other set of circumstances but her own, no matter how desperate!

The garden was a dewy realm of pure beauty, glowing with flowers, dappled with the deep shadows of the oaks, fluttering with birds. In the breakfast room the blinds were already lowered against the lances of the sun; stripes of shade and fine pencilings of light lay across the bowl of roses in the center of the table, the shining silver and glassware, and the pink flowered china.

Mimsie, nearly two years old, sunny-headed and chattering, was in the high chair; the boys' places were empty and had been cleared away; Stephen's chair, at the head of the table, had been squared about; his crumpled napkin and the scattered sheets of the newspaper, as well as the still-smoking coffee cup, bore witness to his departure a few seconds earlier.

Early-morning activities had died away from the big pleasant house, as far as the family was concerned, for Marlys was still sound asleep and the men were gone. But Tony was puttering away in the garden, Fanny's vacuum cleaner was roaring in the downstairs hall, and Wong Foo was in argument with the waiting grocer. Everything was just as it should be, just as Paula liked to have it in her well-ordered days: bedroom windows wide open, debutante daughter sleeping off the delights and fatigues of one more party, telephone all ready to ring with first interruptions and plans for the day.

"Aren't we lucky—lucky—lucky, Deb!" Paula had often said to her sister on these dreaming summer mornings when all had seemed so right with her world. But this morning when Deb came in, stopped to kiss the back of Mimsie's soft little silky neck, and took her place beside the toaster, it was to hear her sister say forlornly:

"I think the whole world is going crazy! I simply couldn't sleep last night."

Deborah folded the pages of the newspaper neatly together, nodded to Wong Foo, who came pottering in with hot coffee, and drank her fruit juice with an inquiring and sympathetic eye upon her sister.

"What now?"

"Steve thinks we ought to go to court this morning!"

"Does?" Deborah's expression sobered, and she sighed. "But it isn't to court, Paula," she reminded her sister, "it's just for a talk with Judge Smith."

"I loathe Judge Smith! He's a sentimental old idiot!" Paula said contemptuously.

"As I understand it," said Deborah, "the Juvenile Court is detaining Mae Singer's children, and she wants to prove that she's a fit guardian for them. The judge simply wants to know what our connection with the case is. Steve said the other day it would probably take ten minutes. There's no publicity."

"It's so *sickening!*" Paula said passionately. "Stephen to be dragged into this sort of thing!"

"I can't see how she gets the nerve to go on with it," Deborah mused, buttering toast. "You'd think Porcher and everyone else would see that she's an absolute faker. She says she has letters from Steve, but she doesn't produce them. She says her lawyer is coming on from New York and he doesn't come."

"Steve doesn't think Porcher believes her for a minute," Paula said. "He's waiting to break the story just before the primaries. Once he has killed Steve's chances he'll drop the whole thing, and her little dream of blackmail will be over."

"There needn't be any publicity to a charge as ridiculous as this," Deb said.

"No; but last night Steve told the whole thing to Phil Saintsbury, and he takes it rather seriously."

"He doesn't!"

"Yes, he does. He said it was most unfortunate coming just now and asked Steve if there wasn't some way of shutting her up. He said maybe the sanity commission could do something about it."

"It's so ridiculous!"

"I know it is. It was ridiculous to have a representative of the Federal Department of Justice walk in here last night and talk about an infringement of the Mann

Act—accusing Steve of bringing Mae Singer to California for immoral purposes! But it means we've got to go to court this morning. Oh, Deb, I get so frightened! If a scandal like this once breaks there'll never be any shutting it up; women will pity me and blame Steve for the rest of our days!"

"We'll get through it. Come along upstairs with me until your Dordy comes after you," Deborah said to the baby, lifting her from her high chair. "What time are we supposed to get to court, Paula?"

"You truly don't have to go, Deb. But of course it would mean everything to me to have you there!"

"I'm going, of course. I've got a note to write and then I'll dress." Deborah carried the baby up to her room and placed Mimsie on the floor with the chess set which had amused not only the young Hazeltines but all the Trezavant babies in its day. Mimsie began to mutter and coo to herself, and Deborah, having closed the door carefully, went to her desk and took from the back of a deep lower drawer a new bottle of purple ink. She then ruffled through another drawer for a sheet of writing paper that chanced to belong to a lot she had all but used up some months earlier and rapidly wrote a short note.

Then she hid the ink again and, folding and refolding the letter several times, rubbed it with her thumb until it looked slightly worn and smeared.

Upon the envelope she had already written the single word "Dave." Putting the letter into it, she crumpled and folded the envelope, too, griming it with a finger tip dipped in pencil dust and finally dropping it on the floor, where she rubbed it about on the rug with her foot.

All this completed, she put the letter in her purse, handed Mimsie over to the faithful Georgia, and dressed herself to go downtown with Paula.

They went to the City Hall, Paula growing more and more nervous every minute. But it was heartening to meet Steve there and to find him casual and cheerful. The wide ugly halls, rubber flooring, smells of ink and dust were familiar enough to him; they went up wide stairs lighted by a great dome of glass high up above them, through passages where patient, dirty, shabby folk sat on benches, and past the marriage-license bureau from which a grinning colored boy and a pretty mulatto girl were just emerging. Everything was grim, smelly, businesslike, and the courtroom to which they were presently and warily admitted was the worst of all. High, staring, dusty windows, dreary dull light, swinging gates, ranged chairs, judge's desk and jury box—"all like a scary play," thought Deb.

The doors were closed to the public—there would be no audience to this preliminary investigation—but there were several persons in the room. Judge Smith was gowned but not at his desk; he stood down on the floor talking to an alert girl secretary who was making notes. Two other men stood near, included in the conversation. Near by Mae Singer and Jay Porcher sat at a leather-covered desk, murmuring together. Seated on a bench was a stout, bland-faced, elderly woman, and with her were the Singer children: two lean little boys and a small girl. A fat baby of some two years sat on the stout woman's lap. The woman looked grave and disdainful; her glance at Stephen was one of cold scorn; she kept the children quiet by constant directions. To Paula it was all like a suffocating nightmare.

"Isn't the law awful, Paula?" her sister said. "We've done nothing, and nothing can be done to us. But isn't it terrible to have anything to do with it?"

"Oh!" Paula murmured, beyond coherent speech. "D'you see Mae over there?" she presently added.

"Oh yes. Looking very chipper, as well she might!"

Mae came over to them, addressed Deborah regretfully.

"Miss Trezavant, isn't this awful? Bringing the children into court; I'd always hoped they'd never know what it was, even. What's happened, when we were all so friendly and fond of each other?"

"I should think you'd know what's happened, Mae," Deborah said dryly.

Not much encouraged by her tone or by Paula's shuddering look of dislike and contempt, Mae persisted, in a pathetic tone.

"If it wasn't for their taking the children I'd never have done it. But rich people can protect their children, and a little widow without any friends or resources, what can she do? And when the *Clarion* said it would pay me for the children's story I went to Mr. Porcher and asked him what to do. You see, I never meant to hurt Paula, but I guess a woman's heart is weaker than her head—"

"I wouldn't do too much talking, Mrs. Singer," Porcher said at her side. "You only have to tell your story very simply to Judge Smith to get full recognition of your rights. I think we're about ready to start."

Judge Smith was seated now at the long leather-covered table that stood below his desk platform; Stephen was beside him. Mae went to her children, took the fat heavy baby into her arms, and, trailed by the others, took her place at the end of the table. Stephen set chairs for Paula and Deborah. The inquiry opened comfortably enough, the fat, white-headed old judge's eyes moving over the company as they spoke in turn.

Paula first. She reviewed the story of her meeting the rain-spattered, friendless, penniless Mae outside of a New York theater and of her offer of carfare. The rest had naturally followed: her interest in the woman's pitiful problem, her help in various ways, her final plan to move the young Singers and their mother to sunshiny California.

The judge listened with no sign of interest. She saw that she was not moving him.

"And you couldn't find in California a worthy family to help, Mrs. Hazeltine?" the judge asked significantly.

"I have helped a good many families here," Paula countered, her cheeks hot. Deborah reflected that the judge was a prominent member of the political party opposed to Stephen, and once again the cruel dependence of the accused upon the whim of those in power presented itself to her painfully.

"You didn't know of your husband's friendship for Mrs. Singer?" the judge asked.

"There was no such friendship!"

The judge drew in his fat cheeks, pursed his lips.

"We have some proof of it here," he said dryly. "I suppose you will agree that it might have existed without your being aware of it?"

"It's always the wife who doesn't know!" Mae Singer's soft voice said emotionally. The judge glanced at her dispassionately, continued his interrogation.

"Mrs. Singer acknowledges her deep obligation to you, Mrs. Hazeltine," he began ponderously when Paula had rapidly reviewed her whole experience with her beneficiary. "She indeed—hum! expresses deep regret for what—for what allegedly occurred. But—ha!— the facts as she relates them are that she knew your husband in New York before she did you. That they met——" He glanced at some notes before him. "They met at a night club," he resumed after a deliberate, unhurried pause, as if he were reading the trains from a timetable; "and on two occasions she met him at a hotel in New York. At that time you were with your brother's family in Baltimore."

"With Tim!" Mae supplied eagerly. Paula, Deborah

suspected, had chattered in her friendly, unsuspecting fashion with Mae during those weeks when Mae was getting settled on the California farm, had mentioned "my brother Tim," and Baltimore, and everything else that interested her and affected her plans. And Mae had remembered.

"That is absolutely not true," Paula said steadily, white with anger.

"Denying isn't proof," Porcher said softly.

"I think that perhaps we'd like to question the boy at this point," the judge said after another interval when he looked down at his papers without touching them, his face as expressionless as a mask. "You're Edgar Singer, eh?" he said to the eldest child. "Suppose you step around here; that's it. You know this gentleman, don't you?"

He indicated Stephen. Edgar Singer, a pale, nervous boy who looked to be nearer ten than his actual age of fourteen years, answered immediately.

"Yes sir. That's Papa, your honor."

Stephen smiled. The blood rushed to Paula's face; Deborah felt her throat thick and dry and her heart suddenly hammering fast.

"That's what you call him, is it?" the judge asked,

still absolutely unmoved. "Tell us when you have seen this man."

"He used to come see Mama out at the San Gregorio Avenue house and sometimes he gave Mama money," Edgar said.

"And when was that?" the judge pursued, patiently and mildly.

"Before Claire-Elise was born."

"And Claire-Elise is the baby, there?"

"Yes, your honor."

"You couldn't get a child that age to lie!" said the stout woman from the Juvenile Home, struck. Mae smiled wearily.

"No, he doesn't lie. He's a good boy. They're all good children. I've lived only for them," she said simply. "I don't say I'm an angel. I know I've done what's wrong. But if love's a sin, then I'm a sinner. I only asked enough from Stephen Hazeltine to keep these babies together, Judge," she pleaded. "I ask forgiveness for everything else, but I want a little home and my children in it!"

"We ask a hundred a month and costs from Stephen Hazeltine, whose own children——" Porcher was beginning. The judge interrupted him.

"We needn't go into that," he said benignly, blowing his nose and touching his big handkerchief to his eyes which had filled at Mae's appeal. "We have the child's testimony here, and we have—— That is your writing, I think?"

He had singled from the papers before him a half sheet of letter paper which he presented to Stephen.

The blood came darkly to Stephen's face. Deb knew this move was unexpected.

"It looks like my writing," he said. Paula turned white.

"I'll read this," Judge Smith said, sighing as if in pained wonderment at the stupidity and sins of weaker men. And aloud he read:

" 'My dear, I go up to the lake this afternoon—little Steve is having a birthday. Still remembering happy time last night. Always yours, Steve.' Did you write this to Mrs. Singer?" he asked.

"I did not," Stephen said.

"You deny it is your handwriting?"

"I neither deny nor affirm anything." Stephen rose. "I think there is no purpose in our staying here any longer," he said.

"I'll look all this over," the judge said to Jay Porcher,

"and we can discuss it again in a day or two. Mrs. Singer is staying here?"

"At the Valparaiso."

"Good. I'll get in touch with you tomorrow or Monday."

Nobody paid any attention to Stephen, Paula, and Deborah as they walked out. Indeed, they were rather studiously ignored. They emerged into a sun-flooded street that seemed strange and garish. For a long time nobody spoke.

They were nearly home when Paula burst out: "Steve, what *possessed* that child!"

"Oh, he was drilled to it. You could tell by the way he watched her face."

"She," Deborah said forcefully, "ought to be in jail!"

"She'll probably end there," Stephen predicted. "Meanwhile—my God, what a disagreeable experience! I wish for your sake it was over, Paula. I've been in courtrooms all my life," he added whimsically, "but I saw a courtroom for the first time this morning! Well, girls, let's get the taste of this out of our mouths until the next step, whatever it is!"

"Oh, Steve, I'm so sick over it! What can they do?" faltered Paula.

"They can't do anything, dear. It's a frame-up, and anybody else but that old dodo Smith would know it. The boy's testimony is just what Porcher would think up as convincing. As if anyone who entered into an intrigue with that woman would encourage the children to call him 'Papa'! Especially if he lived right here in the neighborhood and had a family and a reputation to sustain. No, it's a nasty mess," Stephen admitted, "but I don't see that they can get much further with it."

"But, Steve, perhaps if you gave her a hundred a month, just to shut her up—just now, until you could get some evidence against her, I mean about drugs and drinking and all that . . . ?" This was Paula, beside herself with apprehension.

"That would give her a hold on me that she'd never loosen, dear. That would be an admission of guilt. No; don't you worry about this. I've got Prent working on the New York end; he went on yesterday on the Bingham Will case and I've written him to dig up something on Mae Singer. You girls want to go out to lunch at the country club?"

"Steve, you're such a comfort," his wife said. "No, darling, I can't; they expect us at home, and Deb's got a date."

"Second childhood," Deborah supplied.

"Barry?" he queried. Deborah nodded.

"Not that he knows it yet," she said, "but he's going to be up at Dave Bartlett's old place and I'm joining him."

"Good hunting, Deb," the man said affectionately.

"Oh well!" she said, shrugging and coloring faintly.

Stephen left them, and the sisters went on toward home.

"I wish I were like you, Deb, able to shake this horrible thing off. But I keep thinking that they'll spring something else on us."

"That 'Papa' stuff was simply incredible," Deborah agreed.

"Do you suppose old Smith believed it?"

"The woman from the Juvenile Home evidently did. She simply smacked her lips over it."

"Hateful, pie-faced thing!" Paula muttered. After a minute, with a little effort, she added: "Deborah, was that Steve's writing?"

"It looked like it to me," Deborah answered honestly. "But it was a note he might have written to several persons besides Mae," she reminded her sister.

"How do you mean?"

"Well, to you or me or Marlys—it wasn't dated."

"Oh no, so it wasn't!" Relief was in Paula's voice. "But then how would she have gotten it?" she asked, her face falling again.

"I was wondering that. But you know she went to Steve's office several times while we were at the lake; might have waited for him there and gone through the notes in his basket. It isn't likely, but if Mrs. Rountree had gone out of the office for a minute she'd be investigating like a cat."

"It could have happened that way," Paula conceded, comforted.

Deb dropped her at home and drove back to town, stopping at one of the big, bright, airy groceries where women were pushing little basket carts to and fro among the ranks of canned vegetables and wrapped loaves of bread. When she left she carried a long, well-filled bag to the car, driving at once through the village, past the college buildings, and up the hill to the lane that led to the old Bartlett place. She parked her car by the gate and walked about the house to the open door of the studio.

Barry Washburn was sitting in the big room in an armchair beside the cold fireplace. He had perhaps made some effort to get the place into order, for he had taken off his coat and his hands were dusty, but, despairing of even making an impression upon the confusion, he was now idle. He looked up amazed as Deborah came in.

"Hello!" she said. "You said the other night that you would be up here all day looking things over, and I thought perhaps I was the right person to come and help you."

"Oh, you're awfully kind—you're terribly kind," he began awkwardly, "but I'd just about given it up as a bad job. I haven't the faintest idea where to begin! And yet, you know, I feel as if the dear old fellow wouldn't want all this burned as rubbish and that sooner or later I ought to go over it all."

"It's not so formidable!" She took her hat and her bundles into the kitchen; now she rolled up her sleeves and slipped an enveloping apron over her head. "The first thing," she said, "is to clear this table. We'll put things into three piles. Letters to read, things that can wait, and rubbish to burn."

"Oh, but now, look here, I can't have you getting yourself all filthy with this stuff!" he protested.

"I want to! Ah, please, Barry! You know I was here with Dave scores of times after you went away. When he died I was away—I wouldn't have gone if I'd dreamed that he was going to die—but as a matter of fact, he had no warning either. When I got back everything was locked up waiting for you, and I've not been inside since. I've looked in, longing to make it look the way it used to do, but of course I had no right here."

"Well, of course, if you would help—just getting started," he said gratefully. Instantly they were at work, Deborah quite naturally assuming direction.

"Begin at that end of the table, Barry, and work across to me. These are just advertisements, things that came after he died, I suppose. This is wastepaper—wait a minute, see if you can't find the top of the typewriter and we'll put it on the shelf where it used to be."

A little rubbish fire began to flicker on papers and odds and ends. The table was cleared; chairs were drawn into a huddle, and the long-absent touch of a broom was on the floor; Deborah opened a french window and shook a dustcloth in the midday sunshine. She lowered blinds; a delicious shade and order took possession of the room.

She and Barry had hardly spoken as they worked, except to compare notes on their activities and encourage each other. Presently she straightened up, pushed her tumbled, tawny hair from her flushed, damp forehead, and said with a long breath of triumph:

"There, that looks better! And now for lunch."

"Lunch, of course," he said a little vaguely. "We can—we look like sweeps, of course. But we could go down to the hotel."

"I've brought it, Barry. I'm going to get at it right now, and we'll eat it in the kitchen. You go wash up and I'll get things started. I know that stove of old!"

There was fine oak and madrone wood in the woodbox; it was only a matter of minutes before a frying pan was hot and the contents of the long paper bag were arranged on the table. Barry, returning, made a sudden exclamation that for the first time reminded her of the man of eleven years ago.

"Oh, say, not chicken!"

"Wasn't it always fried chicken?" Her face, flushed and smiling, was radiantly young as she looked at him over her shoulder. "You cut the bread," she directed him; "you remember how? Split it and put it into the oven."

"This," he said presently, when they were seated at the table, ravenously devouring the two-o'clock meal, "is the happiest thing I've done in a long, long time."

His own face looked younger now, without the glasses and with the thick gray hair somewhat disordered. Deborah nodded without taking her attention from her plate.

"And you've had some bad times, haven't you?" she asked quietly.

A silence. Then he answered somewhat reluctantly:

"Yes. Yes, I suppose so. I didn't mean to say this to you," he added suddenly, "but somehow you are making it easy for me to say it now. The hardest thing of all was thinking of you and that I might have hurt you and that you—you were disappointed in me. Don't think," he went on, "that I've come back here—that I'm trying now—my dear girl, all that's over——"

They were looking steadily at each other; the man's face had flushed; Deborah's cheeks were colorless under their tan.

"You didn't write me what happened," she said.

"No, I didn't write. My aunt—I told you of her—she had been the only mother I ever knew. She had been widowed young; she had always wanted a son—I suppose I took that son's place. She had only Marcia—only Marcia. It is so strange to me that I am talking about it!"

In the stiffness, the evident pain of his speech, Deborah could gauge what it cost him. He sat gray and old and broken at forty-six, but his eyes were the eyes of a pleading boy. She said nothing.

"You see, she was dying when I got back," he presently continued. "Marcia hadn't written me that she was ill—didn't seem to realize that it was the end. But Aunt Rose knew. She hadn't wanted to spoil my California holiday, she said. She was leaving me everything—the old house, everything she possessed. And Marcia. When she was in my arms, when she was dying, she made me promise that Marcia never should be sent to an institution. 'Not as just another case,' she said. 'She must have a little house of her own, Barry, her own nurse and cook. She must think it is just a temporary arrangement. I've talked to the doctors from the asylum,' my aunt said; 'they're agreed that it can be done, and you must see to it and stay near her until she is reconciled to it. She must have her victrola and her radio and someone to read to her and to sit with her when the bad times come.' And she made me walk over to the asylum,"

Barry said, "and look at a site for a comfortable little cottage that would still be within the gates of the institution."

"Poor thing!" Deborah said. "And then afterward—after she died—they couldn't make that arrangement? Marcia wouldn't go?"

"No. No, that wasn't it! I've never told anyone. You can't think—you can't think," the man began again hesitantly, "what it means to me to be telling you! I know—I know that I have to go out of your life again in a few weeks. But I will have told you!"

"I want you to tell me," Deborah's silver voice said steadily.

Barry put a lean, long hand over his eyes, pressed it there for a long moment.

"You see, we thought my aunt was a rich woman," he presently said. "She lived extravagantly—four servants, driver, big car, European travel. Marcia always had a nurse, a big woman named Ida, who professed to be devoted to her. Ida's salary of thirty dollars a week hadn't been paid for months. Nothing had been paid. My aunt had told everyone that she intended to put everything she had into annuities for each of them and for herself. Matters were in frightful confusion.

"It all cleared up—or muddled up," he went on with a whimsical smile, "into some fourteen thousand dollars of debt—and Marcia. Poor Marcia, who was so confused and lost, clinging to me, of course. I'd been like a brother all her life. 'You'll take care of me, Barry, now that Dearest's gone. It's you and me now. We're alone in the world.'"

"You haven't been paying off fourteen thousand dollars in these years?"

"I managed it. It is clear now. The last fifteen hundred came from an insurance policy of which Marcia was the beneficiary. We were married, except that it was no marriage. She was a child where marriage was concerned, utterly undeveloped as to any interest in sex. For me, of course, it was only so that I might care for her, live to keep her comfortable and to guard her from outside shocks or criticisms. We had a little apartment in Boston; a woman came in to clean, and Marcia amused herself like a little girl with cooking and flowers. She was never unhappy. But sometimes restlessness would come over her and she would wander away, and so eventually the police of the neighborhood —we lived in a well-populated quarter—came to know her and would help me keep an eye on her."

"And she was never rational, Barry?"

"Never quite. Sometimes we went to faculty dinners in Cambridge—small dinners, where everyone understood. She might be nervous, silent, looking about as if she thought herself watched. Or she might be quite gay and chatter like a child. Then, driving home, perhaps she would say that she was a burden on me and that she ought to open the door and jump out of the car. During the last years I had the gas turned off in the house, except when Mrs. Rourke was there. I knew we couldn't stop her if she was determined to destroy herself, but we did what we could."

"But it wasn't suicide at last, Barry?"

"Yes. She had broken an arm in a fall; I think she had flung herself before a streetcar deliberately, but the story they told me at the hospital was one of accident. She had fainted, they said. She was wretched in the hospital; it was an institution; she called it the 'asylum'; it frightened her. But what could I do except that? One afternoon, while the nurse was out of the room, she very quietly cut her wrists, under the counterpane, and was gone when the nurse returned and saw the red creeping through. They tried transfusions—no use. It was over.

"As much," he finished on a lighter note, "as anything is ever over, Deborah."

The woman's heart gave a great plunge. He was calling her by her first name again!

"The years don't come back," he continued. "I shall always—always feel, somewhere in the back of my consciousness, that the dark little flat is there and the stairs and the door opening upon—I never knew what. Perhaps she would have been working with paper flowers all afternoon and have forgotten the time. Rain falling, perhaps; the kitchen cold. Her voice. 'Daisies are the best flowers, aren't they, Barry? Is it going to be summer tomorrow?' "

Deborah felt a chill. She spoke casually, gathering up the dishes.

"You feel it now, Barry, because it's only ended so recently. But in a few months your heart will begin to heal. You've fought a good fight; you've done the one thing you could do to repay your aunt. I suppose," Deborah said, pouring a stream of boiling water from the big kettle into the dishpan, "if your aunt Rose had known she was bankrupt she never would have asked it of you. I'm sure of that."

"You're generous to be sure of that," he said with a

strange sudden eagerness, his eyes shining; "for it is absolutely true."

"Then you see there wasn't any hate in it, Barry. It was love right through. Hers for you and Marcia, and yours for her. And it's over. Don't try to bring time back," Deborah went on, expertly busy with the dishes, "but go on to new time. Live here, in Dave's house; that's what he would want you to do. I'll find you some woman to clean and cook for you, and you can putter away at your notes for the book. This is a happy place, Barry; you and I had wonderful times here, years ago. We've got the papers into pretty good shape; the rest is mere airing and scrubbing. Why not try peace and sunshine and work and long walks for a while, and see what they do?"

He was sitting at the table, looking at her fixedly.

"Because it seems too much happiness," he said.

"Why too much? No happiness is too much if we can win to it. I think you've won to something."

"I have never thought in terms of it. I have never thought of peace and work and the woods and California," he said. And abruptly he got to his feet and went into the garden, and she saw him pacing to and fro among the overgrown roses and the verbena trees and the sprawling luxuriance of ivy and periwinkle.

After a while she went out and joined him.

"It—it's all so wild," he complained with a gesture. "Dave had it always so—so lovely."

"It only needs pruning."

"I could get someone to do that."

"You could do it yourself. You're no cripple!" Deborah said with a smile.

"But of course I could do it myself! You and I and Dave used to work for hours out here."

"Barry," she said as they wandered about, "all this seems such a—such a surprise to you. What *had* you planned, now that Marcia is gone? What did you *think* you were going to do?"

"I had no plans," he answered, the anxious shadow coming again across the face that had so brightened in the peace of the summer garden. "Someone—Cutter, I think it was—told me that I must work this summer, that idling and thinking wouldn't be good. And the California offer came and I took it. I didn't know whether or not you were here. If I had thought much of that, I suppose I might have thought that, being so much changed myself, feeling myself so different from what I had been, I had hardly to fear being recognized at all!"

It was said haltingly, uncomfortably. Deborah accepted it in silence, and they turned back to the house.

"You have Dave's big workroom upstairs, with his bed and his shower—remember walling that shower with all the old photograph plates?" Deborah said. "And the three smaller rooms and the kitchen downstairs, and of course the big room. You could be very comfortable here. Remember that he used to call it the 'Commons' and hope you'd do some big book there? Why not just let the past, with all its bitterness—and its loss," Deborah went on hesitatingly, "why not let it all go, and begin again?"

"Why not, my best of friends?" he said, taking off his glasses to wipe them and smiling at her.

"Oh, didn't we do a good job?" They had returned to the Commons and stood admiring its order and beauty. The afternoon light entered it tempered by dropped jalousies; the pine floor was clean, the chairs set in their old order. "Oh, and Dave had a special book for you," Deborah remembered suddenly. "He gave it to me the day it was published, with very special instructions that it was to go to you. But I forgot it that day, and I never had another chance. I found it this morning. It's his own book, Barry," she said, coming close to him with the little volume in her hands. "His *Notes on Johnson and Boswell*. He was so proud of it; he had published it himself, but I think he always hoped there would be a second edition, that some publisher would pick it up. And it did get good reviews—surprisingly good. Put it in your pocket. Is my watch right? Is it quarter to four?"

"It can't be!" But it was quarter to four and she had to go.

He walked with her to the car and stood there a moment.

"This has been such a wonderful day," he said.

"Hasn't it been fun? And there's more to do. Painting here and there and getting lights and telephone in."

"You think, really," he asked wistfully, "that I could handle it?"

"Why not? You have to live somewhere. It wouldn't cost any more than any other way."

"It isn't the cost. But somehow I never thought—" His look was vague and pained and tired again after the few hours' respite. "No, I've enough. I'll have Dave's thousand a year when they get that cleared up," he said; "that was all he had."

"It's so lovely." Deborah's eyes lingered on the rich

deep greenness of the garden, with its background of tall trees and crouching hills. Here all was balmy summer warmth and perfume, motionless shadows and flowers burning bright in the sun, but over the western ridge a heavy blanket of white fog was creeping, shutting away the distance, wreathing itself silently into parapets and battlements against the sky.

"If I do come here," he said, "I want you to understand—I wouldn't want you ever to worry for fear that I—I never would dream of——"

"Barry, Barry," she interrupted him smilingly, laying her smooth warm hand upon his as it rested on the car door, "I do understand. Stop worrying about what I will understand! Just take each day for itself, and be grateful that those long, dark years are over and that you discharged your obligation to your aunt to the very end! And come and see us," Deborah concluded, pleasantly and conventionally, as she drove away.

But her heart, she thought, was behaving in anything but its usual fashion. It seemed to her that Ravenshill had never looked so lovely as it did on this summer afternoon. The little college town was asleep on its hills, its tree-shaded streets almost empty, sprinklers flinging lazy arcs of diamonds over the glowing gardens. Oakover wore its homelike air of security and peace. Upstairs windows were open; the wide front door was open, and Deborah could look straight through the square length of the hall to the glass doors at the other end. In the shady north garden Mimsie was riotously engaged with two small friends, the little Bostwick girls; the Bostwicks' French nurse and Georgia Edwards were giving each other language lessons as they watched their charges.

Someone was telephoning in the lower back hall. It sounded like Marlys, but Marlys usually used the upstairs telephone in her mother's room. Deborah quite unconsciously stopped to listen.

It was Marlys, but her voice sounded thick and disturbed.

"But why can't you? If you're so sure you're going to be called, why do you have to study?" Then an uncomfortable laugh and an effort to speak lightly and casually. "Well, because I want to see you. No, truly I do, Condy. Truly. Well, two minutes, then. All right, but I think you're *mean,* and I'll get even with you!"

The last was added in an obvious attempt to appear only a willful, disappointed child grasping at a child's futile threat. But Deborah knew Marlys. Marlys did not often importune boys for favors. Nor did Marlys, emerging into the hall a moment later, wear exactly a child's expression. Her face was white and set until she saw her aunt. Then she smiled, yawned elaborately, and observed that she was dead.

"Have a good time at the dance?" Deborah asked.

"Oh, too good a time!"

"I suppose there was enough racket at the club to keep you awake all night anyway."

"Some of us went rowing up on the lake, and we swam in the Roberts' pool. It was as warm as toast."

"How many swam? Who swam?"

"Oh, Jean and Jim and Condy—only four of us."

"Where'd you get your bathing suits?" Deborah asked as they mounted the stairs together.

"Roberts' lockers were full of them. But there were some girls there," Marlys said, "who went in as is."

"Not really!" Deborah was shocked.

"Well, it was dark, and two of them came rushing down and dived, and they were all laughing; I didn't really see them, but they said that was it," the girl admitted. "I thought it was disgusting and silly. They were swimming around, and laughing and talking with the boys, too, and then two other girls came to the steps with big bathrobes and they ran out and were all wrapped up in two seconds. One of them called out, 'Five dollars!' as if it had been a bet."

"I suppose that is the reason," Deborah said thoughtfully, "that your mother and father feel that they like to know something about the people you are with nights."

"Well, the Roberts are the Arnolds' cousins," Marlys submitted in a subdued sort of voice.

"That sort of thing is so cheap, darling," Deborah pursued.

"They weren't our crowd!" Marlys said with an odd lifelessness.

"You're tired, aren't you?"

"I guess so." They were in Deborah's room now; Deborah was exchanging her dress for a thin kimono and was wandering about in pleasant leisure.

"No date tonight?"

"No."

"But I thought this was the night the Barstows had some plan? Wasn't your mother complaining last week that two nights in succession was too much?"

"Some of them are going up to the Tavern. Nothing special."

"Condy going?" But Deborah knew the answer before she asked.

"No; he'd made an engagement a long time ago to go to the city."

"All the way to San Francisco tonight? He'll be exhausted. Who else is going?"

"It's to meet friends of his from the East that I don't know," Marlys exclaimed, speaking as if her throat were a little sore.

"Well, what you need, chick," said her aunt, "is a simple dinner and a hot bath and early to bed. And I recommend a good scary murder story. There's such a thing as having too good a time. You're not just tired or just sick or just blue; you're all three, and it's a condition described by the word 'jaded.' You're jaded, and rest is the only thing for you."

"I guess so." Marlys' eyes watered; she fiddled with the little jars and trays on the dressing table.

"Life seems very flat after an exciting party," Deb said.

"Oh, *flat!*" the younger woman echoed in a whisper. "It seems as if I had to get back to the Rogerses—and the crowd—and everyone getting ready to do something. It was such fun!"

"There'll be other parties," Deborah said consolingly.

"I know." Marlys was silent for a moment. "You look perfectly beautiful!" she then said, looking at her aunt with new eyes.

Deborah, eying herself critically in the mirror, found no reply. The most potent beautifier in the world was having its way with her and she knew it. Her dark blue eyes glowed; the soft, tawny hair framed a face radiant with an inner joy.

"My old chiffon . . ." she murmured deprecatingly. The fine blue and black and silver stripes of the gown floated about her as she moved.

"You're going somewhere?" Marlys asked.

"No." Deborah had been so conscious of her new bloom that she had deliberately selected an old frock with which to dim it. But it was no use; joy was only the more evident; the glory of youth reborn was shining in every fiber of her. She hid her eyes from Marlys as she left the room.

Chapter Six

"DEB," Stephen said, entering the library as she did a moment later, "where's everyone? I wanted to speak to you without saying anything to Paula."

"Paula took Mimsie upstairs a minute ago; Marlys has just gone to change. She's been asleep practically all day. I changed early because I've been on the go since nine o'clock and I thought I'd take a book out into the garden for a while."

He closed the door; his face was so serious that Deborah felt a moment's uneasiness.

"Is it that wretched Singer woman, Steve? Anything new developed?"

"No. Not exactly. Porcher came to me this afternoon and said that the whole thing would be dropped for ten thousand dollars. I suppose that was to be expected."

"But that's out-and-out blackmail!"

"No, not the way they are working it. He puts it that whatever the truth is about 'our relationship,' as he calls it, she is down and out, she loves her children, she wants a home and security so that she can work——"

"Work!" Deborah put in scornfully.

"I know. But this is their story. There are to be no recriminations and no unpleasantness, but just a friendly out-of-court settlement. She hands me back the note they flashed in Judge Smith's courtroom today."

"Ha!" Deborah said, considering. "But you won't do that, will you, Steve?"

"Certainly not; that would be to put a noose around my neck for life. She'd never stop then. No, we'll just have to face the whole thing and deny everything."

"You think she picked that note out of your desk in your office?"

"I can't think of any other way of her getting it. I never wrote her a line, of course. Never had any occasion to."

"No, of course it wasn't to her." A pause. They were standing in the deep embrasure of a window now, looking out at the garden shrubs. Deborah sighed.

"It was to Ethel Manning, I suppose, Steve?" she said presently. "It was in her desk, presumably."

"Presumably," he said, not turning, still staring out at the garden. Hard red color slowly suffused his face. "That's what I'm afraid Paula will ask me. That's what I'm afraid Paula will find out."

"I told her this morning that it could have been written to a dozen different persons. Marlys—or me . . ." Deborah hesitated. "In all these years," she went on, "Paula's never had the slightest suspicion of Ethel Manning. All she's ever known was that when your regular secretary was away that summer you had this very nice girl in for a substitute. Why, wasn't it Paula who suggested that Ethel come up to the Tavern for the long week end July fourth? And that note, Steve," Deborah continued reassuringly, "needn't say anything to her—needn't give it away. Ethel disappeared—she was wretched about it—she came to me and made a clean breast of it, begging me to tell her what to do, or I never would have suspected it! Just don't ever allude to it again, and I don't believe Paula ever will."

"She asked me, this afternoon, to whom it was written. She said she remembered that birthday and that you and she and Marlys all sent the telegram from the lake," Stephen said reluctantly.

"Paula did?"

"Oh, very lightly. Casually."

"It doesn't sound like Paula," Deb said uncomfortably.

"No. And I wish," he said, "that she needn't hear anything more about it. I wish—you know, Deb," he interrupted himself to say in sudden appeal, "you know how—how short that episode was, what a consummate fool I made of myself, and how—how I felt about it."

"I know. But she wouldn't understand that. She'd feel crushed—you know Paula. You're a sort of god to her, Steve. If nothing more was ever said of that note, if she never heard of it again, we could dismiss it by saying that it wasn't dated——"

"The contents did date it, of course."

"Yes, I was just thinking of that."

Another pause. Then Deborah said:

"The child's ridiculous testimony was really more important than the note, at least as far as any claim on you was concerned. And Paula simply laughed at that. It was too utterly preposterous."

"But she's not laughing at the note."

"No." There was a brief silence.

"I had thought that in what I felt," Stephen said then, "in what I went through when the whole thing broke up, when Ethel went away, had in some way paid for all that. For being such a fool! But it seems one is never paid up."

"Steve, I don't think that note is going to figure in the case at all. I don't think there *is* a case at all," his sister-in-law said. "Admitting that you were a fool, it wasn't like you. It wasn't your sort of thing. Paula's quite right in thinking that you are different from other men, that there's never been anyone else in your heart but herself. When Ethel came to see me—told me about it—I felt that it wasn't you, somehow. I don't know how these things come about; hot weather, maybe, and taking her up to the Tavern, and moonlight. It's been going on a long time, and I suppose it always will. But that

—truly—isn't anything Paula ought to know. It would only hurt her. She's so—so damned *hurtable!*" Deborah said whimsically.

"I know, I know," he said in a thick voice.

"Ethel's married now and living thousands of miles away," Deborah went on. "You did all you could to straighten it out, and it's over. If Mae flashes that note again, you can truthfully tell Paula that you never wrote that note or any other to Mae, and that will satisfy her. You can say, 'How can I tell who I wrote that to? Daisy Pope or Amy Chouteau or someone I'd promised to dine with.' And leave it at that."

"You're a great comfort, Deb," he said somberly.

"Well, the less you make of these things and the less you explain," she reminded him, "the better all round. Come on upstairs now and see the baby a minute before they turn her off for the night. Paula's probably there," Deb went on as they left the library, "and if she says anything about the Singer thing, just reassure her, tell her it's all going to be all right!"

It was dusk now in the library, for the windows faced the northeast and the trees and the shrubbery outside were dense and high. Deborah and Stephen had stood at the north windows; at the further east window a great leather chair had been squared about so that its occupant, were it occupied, might look out at the side garden. The high back of the chair would hide such a person completely from the view of others in the library, especially if she were a small woman, frozen by the first overheard words into the stillness of a statue, shriveled down into half her usual size.

Such a woman rose to her feet when Stephen and Deborah had left the room and staggered toward the door. Paula's face was wan and frightened; her blue eyes were sick. She put out her hand to support herself on the table as she passed it, stopped at the foot of the stairway, and grasped the rail, panting.

"Oh no, no, no, Stevie!" she whispered. And then, half aloud, "Oh, what shall I do! What shall I do?"

After a while, somehow, she was upstairs. Her eldest son, with a book, was sprawled across her bed. Automatically she went to him and drove him away.

"Teevy! Look at my lovely satin cover! Why don't you lie on the couch? Come over here and use these dark cushions; they don't crush up the way the satin ones do. No, no, no, I want you here," Paula assured him as he gathered his uncouth great length to depart. "Only don't lie on the bed. I had these mattresses made over last summer. No, stay with me, dear!" she said in sudden hunger and self-pity, drawing his raw, hard young cheek down to her own. "You're—you're such a comfort to me, Teevy!"

"Your face is dirty," he said, laughing. "Been gardening?"

"I was out in the garden with Georgia Edwards and Mimsie. I wish I was Georgia," Paula thought bitterly; "there's a dignity about being widowed! I wish I was dead."

Going to her desk, she began to ruffle papers, made a telephone call without the slightest consciousness of what she said.

What could she remember of Ethel Manning, the girl who had taken the place of Steve's plain, clever, tried-and-true secretary one summer? Paula and Deborah had had the children at the lake. It had been the summer after their father's death; they had been very quiet. Paula remembered, with a choking dry feeling in her throat, that Steve had been affectionate and grateful when they had returned to town. "Lake week ends were all very well, but since he had had to stay in town and work," he had said more than once, "Lord, how he had missed his family!"

Paula had reveled in his welcome, his love. It was wonderful, after seventeen years of marriage, with a tall daughter and two strapping boys to one's credit, to find oneself still the loved occupant of a man's big arms. She remembered those happy weeks now with a sort of nausea. Had Ethel gone then, or had he been worrying about her, wondering how to get rid of her?

Deborah had known. Paula's cheeks, pale a moment ago, burned suddenly with fever. She took down a dress from a hanger, looked at it, hung it up again. Oh, what was the use of making oneself look pretty, of playing any longer the part of the loved, spoiled, happy little Mrs. Hazeltine! It was all such a farce!

Ethel Manning! She had been a tall girl with a very pale skin and blazing red hair. Paula, happily shopping for the children's summer, had gone into the office once or twice and had seen her there; also she had been up at the lake one Sunday, staying at the Lodge. Who had paid for that visit at the Lodge? Paula wondered, with a thickening throat. She had been down on the beach with the children, racing out to the rock in her trim bathing suit, with her copper hair awash. Had there been a quivering, iridescent light upon that Sunday for Stephen, so dutifully shepherding his wife and children? Paula remembered that she had said of Ethel that the girl looked sullen—"terribly handsome, but why does she look so serious all the time?"

Ha, she had had something serious to think about! The audacity of her, coming straight up to the summer resort where Stephen's family was spending its vacation! But he had probably made her do it! A man of fifty in love was irresponsible!

Paula had been so happy to have Steve there; her face was hot as it all came back to her. "Darling Daddy's going to be with us this Saturday, Teevy. Didn't he say so, Deborah?"

And Deborah, knowing all about it, knowing that Steve was taking tall, willowy Miss Manning to supper, was living in a fool's paradise, had probably said kindly: "Oh, I'm glad Steve's getting away. The town was simply boiling!"

Paula felt that she could not breathe; she was standing in her closet, one hand raised to the line of hangers, her head resting against the softness of silk and chiffon dresses.

"Oh, my God!" she moaned.

"S'matter, Mom?" Teevy called.

"I'm all right." She came out, found Deborah, Steve,

and little Mimsie entering the room. There must be some explanation of her chalky face, blurred eyes, air of bewilderment and vertigo, of course. "I just banged myself against the door," she said, sitting down, the gown she carried trailing on the floor. "No, I'm all right," she added, in response to startled and sympathetic ejaculations, "but for a minute it makes you feel— No, truly I'm all right."

"Muller's downstairs from the factory," Steve said, "and I've got to see him. Sure you don't want a glass of water or anything?"

"I'm fine." Paula was breathing hard. "It was just for a moment."

"Lord, how that can hurt!" Deborah said, all concern. "No, no, Mimsie; that's a no-no!"

"No-no!" Mimsie echoed, not relinquishing the lipstick but rather employing it with guilty haste as a pencil upon the linen runner.

"Stop her!" Paula said automatically. She looked at Mimsie with a sudden thought. Oh, if these thoughts wouldn't come to one!

Three summers ago she and Steve had somehow been very close to each other, after the summer vacation. He had always been the most tender and considerate of husbands; through the days when the children had been small, through a tedious sickness of Paula's that had necessitated weeks in bed, through her father's death and Marlys' accident he had been just Stephen Hazeltine, strong, resourceful, reassuring, infinitely powerful. Nothing had tired him or bothered him or been too much for him to do to keep her from anxiety or burden.

But after that especial vacation there had been a sudden delicious relighting of old fires. They had called it their second honeymoon; they had gone to New York, treating themselves to the best theater seats and the finest suites in hotels, ordering luxurious little meals in the tempered gloom of exclusive restaurants, laughing at each other and murmuring together in lovers' fashion. Mimsie had been the child of that love——

Paula was suffocating again. She walked to the open window and stood there looking out into the lingering last daylight.

When she presently went downstairs it was to meet Bob Muller, foreman of the factory in which the Trezavant money was invested. He was a sturdy, handsome man of perhaps fifty. He and Stephen were smiling at each other as Paula came in.

"Tell Mrs. Hazeltine what you just told me, Bob," Stephen said.

"I was tellin' the judge," Bob said, "that the fellers had a sort of straw vote at the Lodge last night, and they all said—it was unanimous, Judge—that if Steve Hazeltine wanted to run for anything this town could give him there wasn't any party line to it! We aren't strong for Fenelli anyway—after that water-power deal—and it looks pretty good for the judge if he'll give us a chance to vote for him."

"This wasn't just the factory boys?" Stephen asked.

"No, no, Judge, the Lodge!"

"Well, that *is* nice." Stephen glanced at his wife to share his pleasure with her, but he seemed to feel that something was amiss and his manner became somewhat confused. When Muller left a few minutes later he walked with him to his car, returned to find Paula alone in the side garden. Teevy had called down to her from an open upstairs window. "Well, put on your white ones, then!" she called back.

"I had a telegram from Prent about an hour ago," said the judge. "He gets back Wednesday. I don't get what he means, exactly, but he says, 'Landed what I came after and how.'"

Paula's face brightened in spite of herself.

"It means he found out something about Mae?"

"I can't exactly see what he could find out that would affect what she and Jay Porcher, and probably Fenelli, are trying to put over," Stephen said. And impulsively he added: "That dam' note has been worrying you all day, hasn't it? I'm sorry. I can only tell you, dear, that I never in my life wrote a note of any kind to Mae Singer or saw her alone, so that the thing has been faked up out of whole cloth. It's the sort of note one could dash off to anyone—Daisy Pope, if I couldn't keep a dinner date with her; Amy Chouteau—anybody."

Paula was walking slowly toward the house.

"I know," she said quietly, not looking at him. And then to Teevy, who emerged from the side door, "Darling, is that your new sweater?"

"Uh-huh," Teevy answered, kissing his mother abstractedly. "I'm going over to Bill's, Mom."

"Telephone if there's any other plan." Paula jerked the sweater straight on the tall, flat young body, scraped with a fingernail at a spot of dried dirt.

"Bill's mother said to remind you of the cooky sale," the boy said.

"Oh yes, the cookies!" Paula exclaimed. "Deb," she

said to her sister who was just descending the stairs, "do you realize that we have to send six dozen cookies to the sale on Tuesday?"

"Murder," Deborah commented simply, stopping short. "You have a headache," she added.

"Kind of," Paula admitted. Her eyes watered. She felt spent and beaten from shock; she could not shake it off nor forget it. Mounting the stairs, her downward glance reached the open library door; she would never enter that room again without recollecting the horror, the frozen, hopeless horror of those moments when she had been roused from a little time of drowsiness to hear Deb's voice. Deb's voice saying, "It was to Ethel Manning, I suppose, Steve? . . . You're a sort of god to her, Steve."

And Steve: "I thought what I went through—when the whole thing broke up——"

He had gravely decided, of course, that it must end. He had told Ethel so. No woman had ever dropped Steve; it was for Steve to make that decision. Ethel had agreed to go away. "You are right, Steve. We knew from the beginning that no happiness could come of it. Don't blame yourself, dear. I knew what I was doing. And I'm not sorry; I'm glad! I'm glad!"

Paula would have said that she was a woman almost

without imagination. But her imagination was working furiously now. It felt like wheels—wheels going around in her head! She put her two hands up and pressed them against her temples.

"Paula, will you come down a minute, dear?" her husband called from below. She went downstairs again, quiet, dejected, her surprised eyes on the shabby figure of a middle-aged man who was standing with Deborah and Stephen in the hallway. "This is Mrs. Hazeltine," Stephen said. "That's for you, dear."

The man handed her a folded oblong of paper. Paula took it with a bewildered glance for Stephen.

"Nothing to be afraid of," he said, smiling. "It's only a summons."

"A summons!" Paula echoed.

"Judge Smith wants to see us Wednesday morning."

"But—but we're not criminals!"

"No, only for testimony. Nothing to be afraid of."

"I'll not have anything to do with it," Paula said wearily. She tossed the paper onto the hall table and went to the stairs again. Stephen picked up the summons, nodded to the man who had brought it.

Another man came running up the stairs from the garden. Deb said, "Barry!" and her face went April white and pink as Barry came in the wide-open door. He was striding along with something of his old step now; his face was alight under the tumble of gray hair.

"Deborah, could I see you a moment?" he asked.

"Yes, of course. Out on the porch here? It's so delicious outside just now."

They descended four shallow steps and walked along the brick terrace and across the green lawn. Daylight was dying in fragrance and silence and soft shadows. An exquisite stillness hovered over the world; the flowers seemed set in pools of crystal.

"Deborah," Barry said, "I thought I should never say this to you. I came here determined that it would be enough only to be your friend, to see you sometimes, to have a little share in the happiness that you spread all about you."

He was so shaken that she stopped walking and laid her hand on his and smiled up at him.

"And what now?" she said.

"Now," he said, still trembling but speaking with a rush of determination, "now something has happened. Do you remember giving me Dave's book today, the one he wanted me to have?"

"Well, of course," she said with an air of surprise.

"This was in it. I found it! Do you remember this, do you remember writing Dave a note about me? Years ago, probably. Do you remember that?"

"Saying what?" She raised her dark blue eyes to his; she stood before him, slender and straight, her tawny hair, with its few silver strands, falling back from her keen, eager, exquisitely modeled face.

"Saying——" He choked. He had taken from his pocket a trampled and folded envelope addressed in purple ink simply to "Dave." "You can't see this; it's mine," he stammered, "but do you remember writing it?"

"I—yes, I do," Deborah said. And she had the grace to blush, and so made her upraised face even more enchanting.

"You know what it says?"

"That years wouldn't make any difference," Deborah said, tears suddenly in her eyes, "that I would wait for you forever. That if you came back to me an old man, gray and broken, that if we were to have only the last few years of our lives together, I would still be yours."

"Deborah," he said, "I have come back to you old, gray, and broken, but if I could hope—if I could hope that you haven't changed——"

"*You* haven't changed," she said simply as he paused.

"I? Good God," he said, "how could I change! How could I hope—through all those days and nights in that little dark apartment, Marcia's good days and bad days, the work—work—work that kept me sane—how could I think of you as anything but beautiful and young and beloved, and growing further away from me every day!"

"Paula," Stephen said at this moment, at his bedroom window. "Paula, come over here and do a little spying."

Paula joined him, but as he put his arm about her butterfly tininess, in the dear familiar way that had been theirs for twenty heavenly years, she felt a sick shudder go through her. Ethel Manning had been a tall, athletic girl, the sort a man as big as Stephen would find wonderful in the hold of his arm.

"Look down there," he said. His wife looked down and saw two figures seated on the Italian marble bench that Stephen had given her on a birthday not long ago. Deborah and Barry Washburn!

Their backs were toward the house; the man's body was held erect, but his gray head was dropped slightly sideways and rested against a woman's soft mop of tawny hair. From Deb's position it was to be seen that her hands were held in one of his; as the older lovers looked from the window she drew off a little to look up into Barry's eyes. Whatever she said made them both laugh, and presently their cheeks were together.

"So that's that," Stephen said in deep satisfaction. "Well, nobody deserves happiness more than she does!"

"In the first place, I lost faith in him when he slipped away without telling her he was going to marry the daffy cousin," Paula said, not wholly pleased but wholly drawn from her own reflections by this unexpected turn of events; "and in the second place, he looks so exactly what he is, a gray old mole of a professor, that I wonder it hasn't made all the difference in the world to her. But when Deborah once loves——!"

Realization of her own sickening disillusionment engulfing her once more, she turned away and presently descended to the lower floor without addressing her husband again.

But Stephen saw in her changed manner nothing but what was natural in view of the unpleasant threat to his political ambitions; a possible lawsuit, a scandal, warrants and appearances in court; entirely unruffled, he sat telephoning various friends who would supposedly be interested in the mass meeting on Wednesday night.

Could they get Moore to come down from Sacramento? Say, wouldn't it be a good idea to get Corning? He swung tremendous weight.

Paula could not help a comment. At dinner she had to ask him whether it was perfectly safe to go ahead with the senatorship question while the Singer matter was unsettled. In spite of herself his answer reassured her. He was going to act as if it did not exist.

Deborah had gone out to dinner with Barry Washburn. Looking at least ten years less than her thirty-six years, in a red coat and a red hat and a fluffy white gown, she had flashed through the library just before dinner was announced. Her farewells had been fluttered, but joy had shone through them; there had been no explanations, but the family, the younger members of which had rushed to the door to see her off, needed none.

Barry Washburn had been at the wheel of Deborah's small car; she had tucked herself in beside him with no consciousness whatsoever of watching eyes; they had been completely absorbed in each other without a second's delay and had driven away without a backward look.

Even the children's mother had been cheered at dinner and had entered with something of her usual animation into the dinner-table conversation that had followed. Aunt Deb married! It was as strange as if the roof over their heads had suddenly taken unto itself wings and floated away. Aunt Deb married! What do you know, the boys said wonderingly.

Deborah came back to a quiet, dark house at midnight. In a world that floated and shone and sparkled with a million diamonds she crept upstairs, stood for a full five minutes in the center of her room, with the familiar environment of the long years enclosing her and yet with a miraculous strangeness and glamour trembling over everything. Her red hat hung from her fingers, her red coat had slipped from her shoulders; she stood caught in a moment of ecstasy new to her life, rare in any life, and she could not move. Great tides poured over her, washed away, came surging slowly back to raise her to new heights of bliss; an inner joy seemed welling up freshly, inexhaustibly, from her very soul.

"Oh, I shall never have time to think enough about it!" she whispered aloud.

As she stood she became aware of a voice speaking, speaking low but urgently in the quiet house. Somebody talking at midnight?

Brought suddenly back to earth, she stepped into the hall. Everything was dark. Even from under Marlys' door there came no line of light. Yet the tiny trickle of talk was going on somewhere, faintly, behind closed doors, and it was Marlys' voice.

Deborah went swiftly, noiselessly, downstairs, paused outside the library, where the telephone was, pushed open the door. Marlys was talking in the dark. Talking to Condy Cheeseborough.

"I tried—I've been trying all day, but you weren't there," she was saying. "I can't help what your aunt and uncle think—tell them it's about some party—tell them anything! Condy, I have to see you. I can't bear it this way. I can't live with myself! I can't live through another day like today. Will you come take me to lunch tomorrow, so we can talk? I have to talk to you. *Please, Condy*——"

Chapter Seven

To THE odorous dark courtroom a rainy morning was contributing its special element of gloom. Rain splashed on the high, dirty windows; corridors smelled of rubber and dust and rain; doors banged bleakly out of sight, and the stark lights that dangled everywhere had taken on strange halos of murk and mist and seemed only to accentuate the terrors of the place.

To Paula it was all frightful almost beyond enduring. She moved like a woman in a dreadful dream. She had not slept all night, and her small face was drawn and pinched; she kept close to Deborah's side, looking at her sister's face quickly as the business of the morning progressed, as if to claim protection as well as a clue to the significance of the proceedings.

Mae Singer was there with Jay Porcher; the children and the fat, emotional woman from the Juvenile Home were not present, but two or three interested secretaries and law clerks were alertly ready for whatever might develop. Judge Smith, impassioned, virtuous, remote as ever, once more seated himself at the long, leather-covered table, and Porcher briefly put forth his client's claims.

Her New York attorney, he said, was unfortunately detained by illness in that city; seventeen letters from Judge Hazeltine were in his possession and could not be placed in evidence until he was able to travel.

"Why couldn't he send them?" Stephen asked, unperturbed. The hint of a smile twitched at his mouth, a smile infinitely reassuring to the women of his family.

"Oh, I wish we hadn't all gotten into this!" Mae lamented in her soft, fluttering voice. Looking her best in a dark red transparent raincoat, with a conservative red cap and red umbrella, she looked imploringly at Paula. "Couldn't you and I settle this out of court?" she pleaded. "After all, we're both mothers, and why should we hurt and annoy each other?"

"That is a very beautiful and generous sentiment," the judge said heavily.

"I feel it," Mae assured him with watering eyes. "I never can feel hard to anyone! I wish sometimes that I could."

"The upshot of the whole thing is this," Jay Porcher said to the company at large. "Mrs. Singer has suffered injustices since coming—at the solicitation of Judge Hazeltine—from her New York home to California."

"Injustices!" Paula broke in, unable to remain silent. "If you could have seen the home—the slum—she came from! And 'at Judge Hazeltine's solicitations!'"

Stephen moved his amused eyes to his wife.

"He knows exactly what happened," he said with a nod toward Porcher.

"We can sell the story of these injustices to a San Francisco paper for a substantial sum," Jay Porcher pursued. "She has written it, suppressing nothing, and can use with it facsimiles of letters she has received."

"Received from whom?" asked Stephen.

"You know well who from!" the lawyer countered, warming. "She is in desperate need of that money—the newspaper's payment for her story—her sworn story—to establish a modest home for her children. Her husband, to whom she is devoted despite the serious lapse of three summers ago, has been seeking work in southern California."

"I thought he was dead," Deborah put in. "She told us she had taken care of him until he died."

"No, he is—he is not dead," Porcher said after a moment's confusion in which his client had looked at him with a gentle shake of her head and a quiet smile. "He hopes to join her here," Porcher went on, "and together they will raise their children to be a credit to our state. She denies nothing. She admits that, friendless and strange in this new environment, she was tempted beyond her strength by an older man, a rich and influential man in whose disinterested friendship she supposed she could trust. We ask——"

Mr. Porcher looked up from the notes he had been reading. The circle was attentive, although Stephen still wore his amused smile and Deborah's eyes were narrowed to scornful slits. Paula had drawn close to her sister, her face terrified and white.

"We ask that Judge Stephen Hazeltine," Porcher continued, "at whose request she is ready to suppress this story, will compensate her with a sum adequate to cover the costs of this investigation and to start her on a newer and happier road. This is not blackmail, your honor. Far from it. It is merely that, being offered five hundred dollars for a heart story that will wring the— the hearts of every true man and woman in America, she does not feel herself in a position to refuse it. Such a story could not but have a very damaging effect upon any man's reputation, and it would seem to me that a man who proposes to become one of the legislators of our Republic——"

"If any man's reputation could be touched by the rubbishy thing you call evidence," Stephen said, "by such flimsy material as that undated, unaddressed note," he added, indicating the note that Porcher had taken from his pocketbook and was now studying thoughtfully, "no man would be safe."

"No libertine *is* safe in this country of ours," Judge Smith here put in seriously.

"As for the newspapers, they know too much about libel suits," Stephen went on. "If they dared use that sort of thing we should have a sensation every morning.

No newspaper in the world would look at it, as this fellow here knows well!"

He had warmed to a certain feeling on the last words, and his voice rang in the odorous, dismal place.

"Senator Saintsbury differs with you, Judge," Jay Porcher said, holding himself in.

"Senator Saintsbury!" Stephen ejaculated, taken off guard.

"I had a long talk with him on Sunday afternoon," Porcher stated. "He expressed himself as heartily sorry that this unfortunate thing has come up. He agreed with me that it would take less than that to—to disillusion the public as to any candidate for office."

"The bubble reputation," said the judge. "You feel it warm in here?" he asked Mae Singer solicitously.

"I—I——" She had gotten to her feet, her voice choking, her eyes on the big double doors that until a minute ago had been closed upon the hall and its long lines of suppliants outside. They were open now. Two men had come quietly in.

One was Prentiss Talbot, fat, shapeless, well groomed, with his monocle in his eye. The other was a small, square, businesslike person of perhaps fifty.

"If Judge and Mrs. Hazeltine feel that I am making

an unjust claim," Mae said quickly, "I want to drop the whole matter. I will go away and make a home for myself and my children, out of this country, in Mexico or in—in Alaska. I have friends in Mexico who will give me a home. Please, Judge, let the whole thing go. I had no idea how they would feel about it or I never would have brought it up!"

Sheer amazement at this sudden change had kept the group staring at her in bewilderment. No one had had any interest to spare for the new arrivals. But now Paula's eyes wandered, and she said in relief:

"Prent! You're just in."

There was a little confusion in greeting him; it was brief, but it gave Mae Singer time almost to reach the door.

"Stop right there, Mrs. Singer, or Bollini, or Tracy, or whatever you call yourself!" said the strange man in an odd, forceful voice. "There's a cop right outside. He's waiting for you."

Light and hope almost suffocating in their suddenness broke in Deborah's heart, and she saw them reflected in Paula's astonished eyes. Mae returned to the table, addressed the strange man.

"You have nothing on me," she said, her face ashen.

"I may not," he conceded in a leisurely manner, "but the State of New York might have." He took a paper from his breast pocket, looked at it thoughtfully, laid it on the table.

"I want you to know, Mrs. Hazeltine," Mae said rapidly, "that Judge Hazeltine never laid a finger tip on me; I never saw him alone in my life. There's your note." She picked it up from its place on the table before Porcher, tossed it toward Stephen. Deborah took it, looked at it a minute, tore it to shreds. "I don't know what came over me," Mae went on, in the silence of stupefaction that held most of her listeners, "but Mr. Porcher here told me that one way or another I'd get a lot of money and I hadn't any. At first I was going to say that it was Judge Smith who was Claire-Elise's father, because he gave me a lift once in his car three years ago——"

"Good God!" ejaculated the judge, crimson to the gills.

"But I'm not going back to New York," Mae rushed on feverishly. "I'll not go! They can't make me. I can get enough money to get into Mexico. I'll never come back. You can tell them that," she said to the stranger. "I don't know who you are, but it's a dirty trick to trail a girl down when all she's trying to do is live down the past and make a home for her children! Judge Hazeltine," she said, "I trained Edgar four nights to say those things about calling you 'Papa,' but it was he that told me to!" And she pointed at Porcher.

"I'm too busy a man," Mr. Porcher said, rising easily, "to waste any more time on this. My client told me a straight story and I believed her and acted in good faith for the protection of the commonwealth."

"Mrs. Hazeltine," Mae said, "you're so good, won't you help me to get away? Don't believe one word this man says to you——"

"William Bender," the man put in quietly.

"Just help me get away; I'll thank you the longest day of my life," Mae pleaded.

"Whoo!" Deborah said under her breath, on a great gasp.

"Can't we help her, Steve?" Paula asked. Mae sat down and began to cry. Stephen's own eyes watered as he smiled at his wife.

"No, you can't help her," William Bender said. "She's comin' back to New York with me, to answer to a charge of manslaughter. Homicide, anyway. This lady was badly wanted there when she gave us the slip three years ago, as bein' concerned in the death of a boy named Peter Klink."

"I wasn't, I wasn't! I swear to God I wasn't!" Mae gasped. She looked about for Porcher but Porcher was gone.

"You're goin' up the river for a long, long rest, sister," William Bender told her. "They give Lew Cates life. You'll get less becuz all you done was take out insurance on the poor kid and lie about his goin' to his mother in Florida. They dug him up, my dear, and they know all about it. But there's two other charges of children missin'. You must of stepped in," he continued, turning toward Paula, "at just about the minute things were lookin' black for her, and out she skipped for three more years. Come on now, we've got a long trip ahead of us."

"I presume you know," Judge Smith said to the late plaintiff, with pained heaviness, "that charges of this sort against a respected citizen of our country can readily be established as blackmail, and if Judge Hazeltine should care to prefer charges against you, it would give me great pleasure, if your case appeared before this court, to give you the maximum penalty of the law.

"Judge," he said, turning to Paula's husband, "this

has been a very awkward experience for you and for—for Mrs. Hazeltine, whose father, of course, was one of my valued friends. I am glad that we can clear it up so completely."

"Thank you, and good morning, Judge." Stephen hurried his womenfolk away from the polluted atmosphere. Paula clung to him closely. "Who but a little fool like my kindhearted wife, Deb," he said as they descended the stairs, "would have put in a plea for that woman in spite of everything?"

"Oh, we all know Paula!" Deborah said.

Paula, pausing on a step, raised her face to her husband's, and as he tightened his arms about her she linked her own around his neck and burst into bitter crying.

"Why, look here, darling, it's all over, and you've nothing to worry about now except what your wardrobe is to be when we go to Washington," he told her tenderly. "Why, come on, Paula, you never cry when things are all over!"

"That's the only time I d-d-do cry!" Paula stammered, trying to laugh. The dear embrace—the embrace without which she could not live—held her warmly again. The Mae Singer nightmare was over. After all, she was still Mrs. Stephen Hazeltine, with splendid sons, a beautiful daughter, an incomparable rosebud of a baby, prospects of thrilling political days before her. She had so much—she had so much——

They kissed each other, Stephen and she, quite unashamed, quite indifferent to the interested glances that were all about them. Then Stephen dried her eyes, and Paula gulped and laughed and was jumped into the car in the old way, and she and Stephen and Deborah went home to lunch, talking so hard and fast that nobody could hold the floor for more than half a minute.

The impudence of Mae! The miraculous reappearance of Prentiss Talbot at just the psychological moment! The outrageousness of drilling that half-witted little Edgar in his part! The delicious moment when the judge had been drawn into the conspiracy! They went over them again and again, and their arrival at the house was heralded by bursts of laughter. Paula heard her own laughter with a kind of inner wonder. She had supposed that she could never laugh again.

"Steve must never know I know," she said over and over again in her heart. "No one must ever know I know." And so a part of her suffered and died, never to come to life again, but to stab her with sudden pain for a long, long time, and gradually to die away so completely that the very memory of it was lost. Presently Paula would come to feel that she had always known that Steve was like other men; wives had strong compensations in their rights and dignities and privileges, their children and their homes. And whatever he was, her husband was ten times handsomer and kinder and smarter and better than any other man alive.

Marlys was fussing with flowers in the hallway beyond the open door; little Mimsie, with Georgia Edwards in attendance, was starting upstairs, sleepy and sweet and full of good luncheon. Georgia was as interested as Marlys in the story of the morning's events, and for a while they all stood talking together.

"I only saw that Mrs. Singer two or three times," said Georgia Edwards, "but I must say that she impressed me as a lovely, unfortunate sort of person who couldn't possibly do a thing like this! And her name isn't Singer at all?"

"She's used half a dozen names. Tracy and—I forget what they are," Paula said, sitting on the lower step and making love to Mimsie.

"But how on earth did Uncle Prent . . . ?" This was Teevy, an interested listener, now sprawled in a wicker hall chair and attempting to tip it to an angle of forty-five degrees without going over backward on the floor.

"He went to the Charities and they sent him to the police. You could hardly believe it of a city of seven million people," Stephen senior said, "but that's what they did. The police had her history complete—up to the time she disappeared. They showed him Mae's photograph—Prent had only seen her once when he drove out with your mother to call on her at the time she was living in the Santa Clara house—but he recognized her immediately."

Paula lost the thread of the conversation for a moment, thinking of those hot summer days when they all had been so much interested in helping fine brave little Mrs. Singer, and of Stephen's big office with the blinds dropped against the August sun, and of tall, redheaded, creamy-skinned Ethel Manning, so capable and sympathetic at the secretary's desk——

"Mrs. Hazeltine?" Ethel would answer to telephone inquiries. "She's up at the lake with the children."

The pleasant family scene dimmed; the laughter rang false. Paula went in to take the head of the table, and luncheon was served.

"Condy Cheeseborough's coming over about two o'clock, Mother," Marlys said; "he said he wants to see you and Dad."

"Wants to see Dad and me?" Paula repeated, puzzled, but with a bright smile and flush. "What does he mean by that?"

"Well, nothing, Mother!" Marlys said in patient endurance. "He just said would you and Dad be here and I said yes. I wish people," the girl added levelly, "wouldn't always jump at conclusions. It sounds so Victorian, just because a man says he'll call in the daytime——"

"You might have asked him to lunch, darling." Liver and bacon and corn bread and tomato salad were not exactly romantic fare, Paula considered, looking about the table, but there was plenty for a guest or two, and that was something.

"I did. I thought that if he came I could telephone for some ice cream," Marlys said. "I thought you'd all be blue after a session with Mae and need something cheering. But he couldn't come."

"Well, coming at that time, he'll very probably want you to go somewhere with him, to the cattle fair in San José, maybe," Paula said, "and if he does, please don't wear that dress. Wear one of your old brown linens that can crush. I don't know why you have on that new dress anyway——"

"Oh, Marlys, I wish you'd been there this morning!" Deborah put in tactfully. "If you could have seen Mae's face when Prentiss and this New York detective came into the courtroom. To me it was as if the sun had come out in the middle of dreary dark weather. I couldn't believe it at first."

They were back on the Singer case again. They would return to it at intervals all day long, and for many days, and the story of Mae would be dinner-table conversation forever.

"Will she get life, Steve?" his sister-in-law asked.

"Don't imagine so. But whatever she gets, it puts her on the criminal register," Steve said, settling back in satisfaction to await the dessert. "It will make it pretty hard for her to start up any new racket. I'd like to see young Condy Cheeseborough," he added to Marlys, "but I ought to get down to the office to see Prent and discuss that case he went to New York to investigate. He'll probably come to dinner, honey, by the way."

"Good!" Paula said, wishing Steve had not chosen this day of all days to call her "honey." He had called her that on their wedding night. "Scared, honey?" Down at wonderful Pebble Beach, with the sea churning idly in and out of the sharp, long chains of cliff and rock that cut the shore into scallops!

"Prentiss is going to get a nice present from me," Deborah said. "If I could knit those crisscross socks, which I can't——"

"May we come in?" asked a woman's pleasant voice from the doorway. Condy Cheeseborough and his aunt, Mollie Butler, stood in the hall. There was a laughing, eager flutter of welcome; chairs were dragged up, and guests as well as family began an attack on the big platter of apricots, figs, peaches, cherries that occupied the center of the table.

Marlys had jumped up to help with places and napkins; her face was a little pale with a devouring inner emotion, but she showed no sign of it in her manner, except that she was completely unable to manage a smile.

"Condy and I are going the rounds saying good-bys," Mollie Butler said.

"Going, Condy?" the judge asked.

"Enlisted. I talked to the man in San José yesterday," Condy said, "and I go off tonight. Supposedly, that is," he added, with a lenient smile for military regulations. "For, from now on, everything's very hush-hush, of course."

"You go tonight?" Deborah asked. She did not look at Marlys.

"Yes; there's a bunch going off tonight and he got me into it."

"I suppose it had to come sooner or later," Stephen conceded with a sigh.

"Sure thing, Judge."

"I know you said," Marlys began, swallowing, her bright eyes on Condy, "that you thought you might."

"Yep. Remember I said so weeks ago. Well, it was awful hanging around on the diving board," Condy confessed, "but it feels kind of swell to be in. I've got the watch on an olive-drab strap that my Dad wore in 'eighteen, and I don't see how this thing can last long with me in it!"

He laughed his boyish laugh, the big, shining teeth white against his sunburned face.

"We didn't want it and we didn't start it, but we've got to finish it," he said.

"That's the spirit, Condy," Stephen said, departing. The Hazeltine boys had been whispering together now and then during the meal, and the moment their father was gone they burst out.

"Mom, can we? Aw, please——"

Paula looked tentatively at her visitors.

"We've had a movie done of the baby in color, for Stephen's birthday next week," she explained, "and we're all anxious to see it. Have you ten minutes?"

"I'd love it!" Mollie Butler said enthusiastically. "I'm always planning to do that for Jim—Amy did it, you know, way out in China, when the twins were two, and it's—well, it's simply one of our household treasures."

"Darken the library then, boys, and I'll get it," Deborah said. Condy fell in with the plan immediately; he and Marlys drew heavy curtains, pushed chairs about. He understood the movie machine, bent over it with the boys, explained things. Georgia was summoned from upstairs and Fanny from the pantry to share the fun; Wong Foo came pattering in and stood in the dark doorway, chuckling oriental comments from time to time.

Marlys' heart was lead—lead. Condy was absorbed in the management of the film; she would have no word with him alone.

Everyone laughed and exclaimed as the brief entertainment ran its course. Oh, wasn't she delicious! And the butterfly fluttering down to her little hand—was that just accident? Paula, what a wonderful idea!

It must be run a second time, of course. And now Condy joined the audience and slipped into the chair next to Marlys.

"How's everything?" he breathed, looking down at her in the dark.

"Fine," she meant to say casually, gallantly. She knew well that that was what he wanted her to say. And oh, it would have been so wonderful to please him, to win his happy smile again, the smile that said, "You are the sweetest thing on earth!"

But she could not manage it. The muscles of throat and voice and heart refused together. Instead she could only whisper tremblingly, "Condy, you can't go!"

"Why not?" he whispered back, with a very genuine air of amazement.

"Because—because you said that now—now we would always be together," she breathed, the words coming with agony.

"But, darlin' chile, this is war!" He had called her "darlin' chile" before, to her heart's wild joy, but the words stung her like a whiplash now.

"I won't let you!" she stammered desperately.

"I've enlisted. We've not got anything to say about it now." He was coaxing, gentle.

She gripped his hand stubbornly.

"Don't—don't go," she faltered, ready tears brimming her eyes.

He could smile, in his male security.

"But don't you see, I've got to now!"

"No, you don't. I won't *let* you!"

The film ended. Marlys' brothers flashed up the window shades without a second's delay. Then they all saw that her face was splashed with tears and her lips trembling. Ah, she didn't want to let Condy go, no wonder! They had been such friends!

Marlys, dropping her head, ran away upstairs.

"Dear, dear, that's war, isn't it, poor children!" Mollie Butler said sympathetically. "How soon we poor women have to begin to pay! But he's not going to have such a bad time at first, are you, Condy? You see the Fields are right there at Coronado," Mollie continued, leading the way to the porch, "and Harriet's girls are perfect darlings! Condy's known them since he was a baby, Emilie and Yvonne and—what's the little one, Condy?"

"Marianne."

"Marianne. Exquisite child—not a child at all; she's twenty or twenty-one. The movies have been after her since she was in high school, but Walter and Hat won't hear of it. Well, say good-bys, dear. We have to stop at the Houstons' and the Barstows'. They've all—you've all been so kind to this big boy of mine!"

"Tell Marlys good-by again, and tell her to write me," Condy said to Deborah. Deborah's magnificent blue eyes were stern as she looked up at him. The boy's smile died; for a moment he looked confused. Then he shrugged slightly and ran down the steps and got into the car and drove away. Deborah went slowly upstairs.

Winter sunlight, receding over the western hills and meeting the great rolls of the fogs that were tumbling in, slanted across the old Bartlett garden and discovered the mistress of the house busy there.

Deborah was dressed in a pull-over sweater and heavy cotton slacks of dark blue; her head was protected by a disreputable small felt hat pulled on at a rakish angle over the tawny hair. Her face was brown, mud-spattered, happy. She hummed as she worked.

Very little professional assistance had been given the garden since the beginning of the Washburn tenancy, and critical eyes might have found small improvement in it. But to Deborah and to Barry, when she pointed out the results of their work, great progress was to be seen. The brick paths had been cleared and swept, and there had been drastic pruning among the overgrown shrubs and rosebushes. But there was still much to be done: persimmons still hung in orange balls upon the leafless trees; apples rotted in the grass of the hilly strip of orchard; oak leaves lay in heavy drifts against the fences and the porch steps.

Deborah, straightening herself, trowel in hand, to rest her back, looked about her domain and decided that she loved it all and that she hoped it would not ever be too thoroughly ordered. She loved the dormer windows upstairs and the long, low-ceiled bedroom to which they belonged; she loved the shining panes of the parlor that reflected this afternoon's red sunset mingling with the fog and showed hints of mahogany chairs and mellow rugs and an old square piano when one stood on tiptoe in the path and peered in. She loved the long room that was Barry's workroom, and her living room, and the center of their living plans; the room from which the broad brick chimney rose, whose enormous, small-paned high windows let the light in from three sides. It had a low porch that jutted into the garden, this room, and old Ruggiero now was piling more wood and more wood on this porch for the afternoon fire.

Her affectionate eye roved about the place. There was a little collapsed hothouse with the beautiful acanthus leaves of artichokes spouting up against it; there was a sloping paddock where two saddle horses were standing in exactly the same position, like book ends, their necks resting against the top rail of the fence. There were odd curving bits of path that ended at the bare whips of berry vines, and odd small gates half buried in shrubs, and odd small lots of tumbled-over flowerpots and rakes picturesquely heaped against old brick walls. Majestic oaks towered here and there, interspersed with smaller trees; peppers trailing pink necklaces and scenting the air with pungency; eucalyptus trees foolishly bursting into tassels in the warm November sun. A stout-legged worn plank table was bedded firmly in earth under a grape arbor; the grapevines were shriveled skeletons now, through which the sunlight made a bold pattern. Chickens clucked behind wire fencing; an aged Chinese in coolie blue came out from the kitchen and flung them the contents of a tin pan.

"Enough is enough!" said Deborah aloud.

She went in at a narrow side door and mounted narrow stairs. There were windows all the way up the stairs; red roses had been pressed against the windows when Deborah had first come to the house as mistress. She would always see them there, fresh and crowded and glowing, even when as now the vines were almost bare.

The long, low bedroom was a little chilly, but the bathroom, walled with old photograph plates by three friends working together on a happy day years ago, was warm, and Deborah was quick with her shower and change. Comfortably refreshed, she went down to the big room and interrupted the work of the gray-headed man at the big table. She interrupted it by going to stand beside him, and he put his arm about her and drew her down until their cheeks touched.

"Heaven," he said simply when she freed herself and moved about the room, picking up a magazine here and moving a chair a few inches there, lighting a lamp, drawing a shade. And "Heaven!" he said again when he left his papers and typewriter and came to build up a roaring fire and sink into his big chair beside it.

"Oh, this is good!" Deborah said. "And here's tea!"

Here was tea brought in by the old Chinese—tea and

sandwiches and tiny meringues spread like butterflies with pink candy eyes. The round tray was placed on a leather hassock, and Deborah officiated without leaving her chair.

"Yes, this is heaven," she agreed, biting into brown bread and cream cheese. "But it isn't more, materially, than hundreds and thousands of people could have, so the question is, what is heaven?"

"Heaven for me is you," Barry said simply. "Seventh heaven. Heaven beyond anything I ever dreamed was in this world. There isn't one moment in my life from the time I wake up with your head on my arm——"

"Or yours on mine," said Deborah. "Or me shaking you and saying, 'Do light the stove, Barry, or I'll never get up!'"

"Breakfast here by the fire or out under the arbor—I'll never forget those first breakfasts last August," Barry said. "Breakfast is heaven. If I have a class, it's heaven to have you drive me there and say that the corn is getting rather poor and that crabs won't be in until next month. It's heaven to come home to this room and you—heaven, heaven, heaven!"

"It's love," Deborah said seriously. "If there was enough love in the world to go round there'd be enough of everything else. Because brown bread and butter are a feast when it's just we two."

"Deborah, do you suppose that if I hadn't found that note you wrote Dave I ever would have gotten up the courage to ask you?"

"I don't know." Deborah studied the sandwiches thoughtfully, selected one from which lettuce and tomato were protruding. "I've often wondered," she admitted innocently.

"Why don't you ever use violet ink any more? You always used to use it, years ago."

"Maybe I was kind of sick of it for a while. Maybe it reminded me of the little notes I used to write you and Dave," Deborah said. "But I have a bottle around somewhere, and I must begin using it again," she added. "Only of course you'll not get any notes now because we'll never be parted again."

"If I had known what all this was going to be," Barry told her, "I would have chanced asking you, just as men take a desperate chance when it's a toss-up between life and death. I know now what I would have missed. But when I got here I was so tired, so depressed, so old, that instead of ten years younger you seemed like a child of mine!"

"It seems quite impossible that we can go on like this, Barry. Day after day and hour after hour getting nicer and nicer. Tonight, alas," Deborah said, "we'll have to make an effort and go down to Paula's. I was there until after three—terrific goings-on. Radiomen in the boys' rumpus room downstairs and food for hundreds laid out and people coming and going. I had a few ideas about sandwiches and cookies, but no—Paula had a caterer come in and fix up long tables and do everything. By the way, you'd better finish the sandwiches; we're not having any dinner here. I knew that we could eat there."

"Let's walk, Deb. I love that walk."

"Oh, let's walk! It's not a mile, and you've been in the house all afternoon. That'll console us for having to waste an evening."

"I don't have to dress, I suppose."

"Oh, heavens, no! It looked like a railroad station when I was there, everybody surging about. No; wear what you have on. I'm going quietly to sleep here—I'll be ready in an hour—I told Paula about seven."

When they were walking down toward the village under the early cold stars she said:

"Isn't the night friendly?"

"This whole town is friendly. College buildings and big trees and little houses with lights shining out under the trees. I love it. Now that the students are back and all the little cars parked outside the candy stores and movies on University Avenue, it seems—American, somehow. Youth coming to the sources of learning. They used to do that in Europe a thousand years ago. There's something fundamental about it. I hope I never get dry and academic, Deb, but I do like it."

"You'll never get dry and academic. You're getting humaner every moment. Barry," Deborah said, linking her arm in his and bringing her shoulder close, "I am trying to make a choice and I don't really know what I want."

"For Christmas, dear?"

"No, for early summer. Sometimes I think it would be so nice to have a proud little girl with Alice-in-Wonderland hair hanging on her shoulders and pinafores, and sometimes I'd love a sturdy, rough little boy who'd spill things. Of course in time we could have both——"

"Are you telling me something, Deborah?" He stopped, in the blackness under great trees, but a faraway street light caught a bright glint from her eyes as she faced him. Barry's voice was shaking; he held it low.

"I s-s-suppose I am," she said with an unsteady shred of laughter. "Are you surprised?" she added in a silence.

"No. I have thought in the last few weeks—sometimes in the mornings, at breakfast——

"But this is too much," he said after another silence. "This—this is too much."

"You're not sorry, Barry?"

"Sorry? To have a child of my own! A son—a daughter like her mother——"

"Like her father," Deborah said firmly, against his coat buttons.

After a while they went on down to Paula's. They were late, but nobody in the house was in a mood to notice that or anything else. Every light was lighted from attic to cellar, and every door was open. Strange men rushed about with bulbs and snakes of wire; waiters carried chairs here and there. In the hallway Stephen was in conversation with two important-looking men; Paula, pretty and flushed, with a new hair-do, entertained a group of women friends in chairs around a drawing-room fire. Fanny was in evidence, Georgia

Edwards; the three older children were in a wild state of excitement.

In the dining room long tables were loaded with sandwiches, cold hams, two great roast turkeys, salads. Wong Foo, who was to go to Washington if and when the family went, dispensed coffee. Stronger drinks were on tap downstairs where reporters and radiomen congregated. Three telephones rang constantly, and a loudspeaker, connected with one of the newspaper offices downtown, droned out the latest reports. Young men stood about with rolls and chunks of meat in their hands or laid coffee cups or glasses on the window sills or stairs. Cigarette and cigar smoke spiraled through the warm air and floated up in blue clouds to the ceilings.

There was a big blackboard in the library, its surface divided into the state's congressional districts. Prentiss Talbot and several other men were working there with chalks. They erased, sneezed on chalk dust, changed figures. Every little while one of them shouted, "Steve, it's all one way. It's in the bag!"

Everyone knew it was in the bag. The unfortunate Fenelli, obtaining by fraud the rival nomination, had been recently exposed. Fenelli had been putting up a furious verbal fight, hiring bands and filling pages of advertising matter, but the odds were heavily against him, and it was conceded even by his supporters that the fight was lost. At eight o'clock Fenelli had declared he would demand a recount. There had been overflow meetings in Stephen's interest for weeks; the great Fenelli mass meeting, scheduled for the night before, had been canceled.

Marlys naturally occupied a prominent place on this important evening. She wore a snug white satin frock with little bursts of scarlet ostrich feathers here and there. Her hair hung loose in soft curls that tumbled and blew about in a manner presumably attractive to all the young men who were officially busy in the house; radio operators and reporters and cameramen had a way of stopping on their busy comings and goings to chat with the daughter of the house.

She was thinner than the Marlys of six months ago—older. Just as the impalpable bloom of a long-extended girlhood finally fled Paula's cheeks, leaving in its place a charmingly soft maturity, so something had forever escaped from Marlys' beauty too. Something essentially youthful, some glamour of adolescence and childish daring and confidence, was gone. There was a faint sign of hardening now and then, about the mouth or in the corners of the eyes; there was a faint sign of suspicion and wariness.

But these slight changes were only visible to eyes that watched her as closely as did Deborah's eyes. Deborah had seen the long weeks of autumn taking their toll; she had known what letters the postman did not bring; she had watched Marlys fly to the telephone for the call that was never the right call. Condy had never written; Marlys' carefully contrived meetings with his aunt or uncle had brought her no personal message. Sobered, a little quieter, a little harder, Marlys, to the general circle of her friends, might seem to be only growing up. But Deborah knew. Marlys had won to a certain philosophy, but it had been dearly won.

Paula, too, was changed. If she had found that her idol had feet of clay, he was still her idol. She could not live without Stephen; his big hand under her elbow when she crossed the street, his quiet solution so ready for her hardest domestic problem, his praise, his love, his admiration were her daily bread. She wished—at first furiously, with a despair that had only slowly won to patience and resignation—that Mae Singer's detested name had never entered their family annals, for then she would never have known of the Ethel Manning episode.

But much was left. Pride was left. Paula knew already that she was too proud ever to tell him that his secret was known to her.

"He's too kind and good and wonderful in other ways, in every way," she said over and over again in her heart, "for me ever to hurt him! It wouldn't change what's past, and it would make him unhappy—he'd not forget, and he'd know I wasn't forgetting. It's much better as it is!

"Only—only"—the thought would come, and with it a sudden chill at her heart, a sudden watering of her eyes—"if he'd only told me himself, let me forgive him, let me say I understood! When I've failed him, forgotten the tickets or something, or mislaid some of his important papers or not given him a telephone message, he's always been so kind! And I could have been kind too—I would have been kind!"

And she was kind to him now, tender and considerate and patient. It was a kindness and a patience that went deeper than anything that Paula had ever felt before. She felt it enriching, strengthening her own character. But she knew she would never go back to glad, confident mornings again, and deep in her being there was a sense of eternal loss.

"Mother has taken that Mae Singer matter pretty much to heart," Marlys said more than once to Deborah. "And d'you know why?"

"Why?" Deborah had countered in some trepidation.

"Because she dared say anything against Dad," Marlys had returned confidently. "Mother wouldn't have felt half so bad if it had been anyone else. But *Dad!* And then another thing," the girl had continued. "Mother brought this onto the family. Of course she did it quite innocently, but it was her doing, and I think it burns her up. She never says anything about it any more, and she has a sort of motherly attitude toward Dad that she never used to have. Notice?"

"I think I do," Deborah would agree thoughtfully.

On the other hand, Deborah had had to hear Paula's confidences regarding Condy.

"Do you agree with me that she really cares for him or *did* care for him, Deb?"

"Oh yes, it went pretty deep."

"She's so young," Paula would say, unworried, "that I'm not sure but what it was a very good thing for her. It's developed her, made a woman of her, really. Of course by the time I was her age I was already in love with Steve——"

And Paula might stop for a sharp little sigh that was entirely new in her references to her husband.

Deborah never noticed the sigh. But sometimes she spoke in quiet disapproval of Condy.

"He's never written her, Paula."

"I know. But I don't know how busy they keep them in camp, Deb. And I suppose he'd have to write to so many! I don't know that she's written to him, do you?"

"Probably not," Deborah would say untruthfully. She knew that two letters, and after a long interval a third, had gone from Marlys to Pensacola where Condy was in training. But Marlys had to be protected from any family comment about that.

However, Marlys and Paula were both in brilliant looks and spirits on this great election night, and both were having their fill of flattery and excitement and activity. The house was given over to laughter and interruptions and messages and feasting; when Paula found anyone who had not dined she led him straightway toward the sandwiches and coffee with a little proprietary air of concern that, contrasted to her diminutive size and the height and weight of the person she had in tow, was infinitely engaging and motherly. Stephen kept his boys racing on errands for everyone: "Put Mrs. Barstow's coat somewhere, Teevy." "Trez, run upstairs and take that telephone call and tell them to put it on down here."

He was very simple, very natural, but of course he was inwardly excited and tremendously gratified, too, as old friends and neighbors streamed through the house and anxious and nervous hopes strengthened into a certainty of victory. Precinct after precinct turned in the same story: Hazeltine, nine hundred; Fenelli, two hundred and fourteen; scattering, eighteen. Hazeltine, five hundred—Hazeltine, three hundred——

Pretty, quiet little Diana Briggs and her brother Ken were there, with big, awkward Roger Messenger, whom Marlys had once called "the perspiry boy," in attendance. And Di wanted Marlys to know first of all that when Roger graduated from medical school in June he and Di were going to be married. His look of solemn adoration and rapturous bewilderment when Marlys congratulated him, and Di's look at him, made Marlys thoughtful, although all that she said to her aunt when they chanced to be alone for a moment a little later was that she had never supposed that Di would be married before she, Marlys, was.

"Di's two years older than you are," Deborah said, sure in comforting inspiration.

"That's true," Marlys admitted.

There was other news tonight too. Condy's aunt and uncle, the Butlers, were there. Jim Butler was one of the men most active at the blackboard. Mollie fluttered about greeting friends and assuring Paula that she was going to adore Washington. Mollie had once visited Washington for several weeks.

"Oh, and we had a letter from Condy," Mollie babbled happily. "He's got his wings, you know; he's an ensign now. He says he thinks he'll be ordered to San Diego soon—of course no details, so we may see him again. And what do you know about his engagement to Vonnie Field—perfectly adorable girl, European education, speaks three languages, all that! We're awfully pleased, because it means a sort of settling down for Condy. He'll be away for a while, but when the war's over it means an anchorage for him. She'll have something of her own, from the Castle grandfather, of course; it's just ideal in every way!"

"They'll be married before he goes?" Deborah asked, slipping an arm tightly about Marlys who stood beside her.

"No, the whole family's coming out to San Diego for a real Navy wedding," Mollie said. "Condy wrote, 'My sisters-in-law would never forgive me if I gypped them out of being bridesmaids, to say nothing of my wife raising hell about it.' It did sound so grown up and responsible. 'My sisters-in-law and my wife!' "

"You must write him, Marlys," Deborah said brightly. "We must have his address. Mollie, come over here and write it down. And, Marlys, will you run upstairs like a darling," she added, "and see if that's catcalls outside or Mimsie waking up?"

A few minutes later she followed Marlys to the nursery. The girl was sitting in the dark beside Mimsie's crib, looking out at the night. Already the Hazeltine garden was filled with moving figures; a rocket went up, and from unseen groups everywhere there came a prolonged "Ah-h-h!"

"Aunt Deb," Marlys said in a composed voice. Deborah's heart felt an uprush of relief.

"I was afraid you were crying, dear."

"No," Marlys said lifelessly. "Aunt Deb, does it seem to you a strange six months—these past six months?"

"As you grow older," Deborah said, "life fills up, somehow. Perhaps it's because when we're babies we think of nothing but ourselves. Then gradually other lives begin to interest us; we feel sorry for something that worries Mother or we sympathize with Dad or we hope something for a brother, and so we widen our capacity for loving. And loving is pain, Marlys."

"Not if you don't compromise," Marlys said, speaking a little thickly.

"Less, of course, if you don't compromise."

"Six months ago the horrible Singer thing hadn't broken," Marlys began presently, after a pause during which she had held tight to her aunt's hand. "Senator Saintsbury hadn't suggested that Dad run for the Senate. Barry hadn't come back and you hadn't been married. And I'd not met Condy."

"And now Washington for all of you," Deborah said cheerfully. "And new friends, Marlys, new experiences. Take it all as if this Condy experience had been only a sharp lesson, something that one's sorry for and won't be deceived by again, something that makes one wiser."

"I know all that," Marlys said wearily. "But what I was thinking of," she presently said with some little difficulty, "was this: Would a man—I mean if he was in love with someone else, marrying someone else—would he think it was smart to tell her—to make her think that girls liked him——"

"No, he wouldn't," Deborah said decidedly. "In the

first place it isn't very much to his credit, so he won't tell her now when he wants her to think he's perfect. And if he gets boasting after they are married," she continued serenely, "she won't believe him. So that if I were you I'd put that thought right out of my mind."

"You can't put things out of your mind, Aunt Deb."

"No, but you can turn them to good. You can turn all this to good, Marlys," Deborah said in a more serious tone than she had ever used to the girl before, "by determining that you are going to be a perfect woman. Not merely attractive, but perfect. You're very unhappy now; you think your heart's broken. So this is a very good time to start—start from scratch as it were. This is the time to take up some useful war work. You're a leader; you can naturally attract other girls to it. Keep up your Spanish; always be gentle with the boys, think of your father and mother before you do of yourself, and when you do pick out a man be sure he's good and fine and ready to make you the right husband.

"Then have a lovely home, with sweet children in it, and perfect your life as if it were a play you were writing, always to be more and more polished in every detail.

"And after a while, Marlys," Deborah went on as the girl, still holding her hand tightly and crying now, did not speak, "everyone will begin to feel that young Mrs. Smith or Jones is an exceptional woman, reliable and clever and beloved. In that way you'll win after all. For if I know anything of young Ensign Cheeseborough," Deborah finished on a lighter note, "he's *not* destined to make any woman or himself happy. He'll drift back into your life someday, divorced probably, discontented, and you'll be so far above him, Marlys, so busy and happy and beloved, that you'll have no self-consciousness about it at all."

"I hope I never see him again," Marlys said darkly. "And I hate Mrs. Butler; I despise her!"

"I never was especially fond of Mollie," Deborah said dreamily, and Marlys laughed shakily.

"And never to speak of it, Aunt Deb?" the girl said when they were in the upper hall.

"Never. Not to anyone. To forget that love affair as if it had never been," Deborah said firmly. Marlys pulled her back for a kiss before they went downstairs.

They were just in time to hear Ken Briggs, setting down a telephone, rise to his feet for an announcement.

"The following message has just come from Joseph Fenelli to Judge Hazeltine. 'Congratulations upon your election and best wishes for your years in office.' "

Cheering broke out everywhere, and a band stationed in the front yard burst into violent action. Stephen was kissed, his hand was wrung, he was pushed about by the milling throng. Little Paula was picked up and stood upon a chair, from whence she clapped and laughed with the rest.

After a while Mimsie was brought downstairs in a state of dewy-eyed amazement, and everyone made room for the photographers. Stephen sat in his big leather desk chair, with Paula at his side; young Stephen stood behind him, and Trezavant was on his other side on a low hassock. Marlys draped herself gracefully over one arm of his chair, and little Mimsie sat on her mother's lap.

"Let me get this, left to right," one of the reporters said, scribbling. "Mrs. Hazeltine with the adored baby of the family, Deborah; the Senator; Miss Mary Elizabeth Hazeltine; George Trezavant Hazeltine; and, standing, Stephen junior. That's right. Try 'em another way for the Associated Press, Bill."

R01143 19136